MAGIC BOOKCASE

THE PREHISTORIC PROLOGUE

MEGAN MURRAY

First published 2017
by Megan Murray

Copyright © Megan Murray 2017

ISBN : 9781787231542

Printed and bound in the UK

For Mum, Dad, Emma and Callum

my roots and wings,

everything begins and ends with you

For my niece, Penny Jane

my sunshine and smiles,

the stories are all for you

And for Scotland

my soil and soul,

and a place full of magic

CONTENTS

Author's Note

I hope you enjoy reading the adventures of Maggie and her very clever Grandfather as much as I have enjoyed writing them. The language I use is quite advanced; it will stretch your vocabulary. To help you along the way I've written a glossary for the challenging words (these are <u>underlined</u>), at the end of the book, organised by chapter.

The history of Scotland is a fascinating subject; I hope I've managed to do it justice and provide an introduction for you to the many interesting tales that make up our collective-past. As Granda explains to Maggie, what we know of history has been interpreted in many different ways, but importantly, by *modern* people. We have no real way of knowing the absolute truth of what took place in the past; it will always be a matter of filling in some of the blanks for ourselves. I think this is more exciting anyway, and these Magic Bookcase stories are my interpretation of the many wonderful tales that make up the history of our country.

I've always thought that books are magical, and have always loved getting lost in them. This was my chance to explore what would happen if we could actually get inside them. I hope you enjoy the adventure. The most important thing is to always keep reading!

PROLOGUE

Maggie is a small girl from Gourock, a town on the River Clyde, not far from Glasgow, in Scotland. She lives with her Mum and Dad but a few times a week, she visits her Grandfather. While most children visit their grandparents and perhaps go for walks to the park, or have cakes and cups of tea in the kitchen, or maybe watch some TV, Maggie and Granda go on time-travelling adventures with the help of a bookcase that sits in Granda's front-room. I'm sure I have your attention now.

CHAPTER ONE

Maggie's tenth birthday had arrived at last. She'd been counting down the days, even though her Dad had told her to 'stop wishing her life away' and enjoy the build-up instead. Maggie hadn't managed very successfully, and had been as impatient as ever to get to the sixteenth of June and the weekend that followed. She was having a party at the local laser-tag arena and she simply *couldn't* wait. The day of her birthday had been lovely so far – everyone had sung 'Happy Birthday' to her at school and she'd been allowed to wear the teacher's special birthday badge. Granda had collected her at home-time and they were waiting for Mum and Dad to finish work before they had Maggie's birthday tea.

After a snack, Granda asked Maggie to go and sit in the living room, saying that he had a birthday surprise for her. Maggie bolted for the big square room and sat on the edge of the sofa in delighted <u>anticipation</u>. Granda came in with his West Highland Terrier, Wally, under his arm and settled him on the wide window-ledge, (his favourite look-out spot), without saying a word. He looked particularly serious and Maggie was suddenly worried. Granda was very old – seventy-two years old, to be precise – what if he had some bad news for her? He'd said he had a *surprise*, surely that meant there was nothing to worry about?

'Right, Maggie-Moo, here we are at your tenth birthday...' Granda began, lowering himself heavily to the couch beside her. His solemn expression hadn't fully lifted, but he smiled a little as he said the words. 'I have something very exciting to share with you, something that might sound a bit strange, or even a bit crazy...'

Maggie held her breath; what on earth could this be? After a few seconds in which Granda looked like he was still trying to decide how to share this exciting something, he spoke:

'You know my bookcase–' Granda gestured to the huge piece of furniture in the corner of the room. 'Well...' he puffed out his cheeks. '...see the thing is, Maggie, my bookcase isn't just a normal bookcase...It's *magical.*'

Of all the things Maggie had been expecting, this was possibly the last. She was sure now that Granda was having a laugh, a carry-on, just pulling her leg. Yet his face was still very serious, not even a hint of his usual <u>mischievous</u> grin to give the game away.

She looked to the bookcase, towering high over the living-room from the back corner. Maggie had always been aware that Granda's bookcase was a bit unusual; it was massive, made of solid, dark wood and was very old, having been passed down through the family for Maggie didn't know how long. It had <u>ornate</u> carvings on its front and sides, the wood worked into beautiful swirls and flourishes, twisting thistles and Celtic knots. Four <u>intricately</u>-carved animals stood proudly on its front; two at the top and two at the bottom – a unicorn, a stag, a seal and an eagle. Maggie had loved looking at them since before she could remember, had imagined them galloping, leaping and flying like real animals. They almost felt like they were old friends, somehow, the same way the books themselves were familiar and comforting to her. She and Granda read together all the time: reading was one of her favourite things to do, even if some people at school teased her for it sometimes. She really didn't care, much.

Aside from its impressive decorations, the bookcase was positively packed with books, their spines standing neatly side-by-side, some thick and tome-like, others thin paperbacks. Some of the books looked as old as the shelves they sat upon, others were very new, their colours popping almost garishly next to their faded neighbours. It was the pride of Granda's front room, his bookcase, but seriously, it was *magical?* Maggie sat blinking disbelievingly at Granda's still-solemn face. He seemed to be serious!

She was suddenly worried again. She wondered if Granda had perhaps begun to 'lose his marbles', a phrase she had heard her Dad use in reference to their next-door neighbour, Mrs McNicol, who had a great many garden gnomes, and could often be found in the garden, talking to them.

Mrs McNicol's daughter didn't visit too often and Mum told Maggie that it was therefore up to them, as her neighbours, to look out for her. Mum took her shopping a couple of times a week and Maggie helped Dad to keep her garden tidy, mowing the lawn and weeding the paths. She often gave Maggie sweets and Maggie enjoyed listening to her talk in her crackly old voice about being a wee girl in the war-years. She told her stories about the rations, when sweets had seemed rarer than gold-dust (especially Mrs McNicol's favourites – Pear Drops – which Maggie had tried and liked very much). Maggie liked the old lady, and she in turn seemed to enjoy

Maggie's company, even if her football constantly flew over the fence, often putting her gnomes in serious danger.

However, Maggie had heard Mum and Dad talking in low voices in the kitchen one night, saying that eventually she would have to go to a home. She heard them use the word 'senile', which sounded like something painful and Maggie was suddenly worried that Granda might soon have to go to a home too.

'Magic?' she asked, drawing the word out slowly, mind still working hard to sort out the jumbled thoughts that Granda's announcement had triggered. She searched the face she knew so well, still wondering if he was just kidding her on, a birthday prank before he pulled out a brightly-wrapped gift and ruffled her hair in amusement. But his brow creased in impatience.

'Yes, lassie, magic, what's with the <u>sceptical</u> face?'

'Well, it's just, Granda, how can it be magic?
Does that even...even exist?'

'Exist? Course it does,' Granda gruffed in reply,
'How do you think your presents end up under
the tree every Christmas? Where did your wee
milk-tooth disappear to last month? There's
plenty of magic to be found all around you if you
just open your eyes and see it...if you open your
mind enough to believe it.'

He had punctuated this sentence by prodding
Maggie's forehead with his index finger. Granda
had very large hands; this was nothing to be
sniffed at.

'But why are you only telling me now? Maggie was still a little concerned.

'If you're old enough to have piano lessons, you're old enough to know about the bookcase – it's all magic really, music and books, is it not? I was your age myself when I found out, and had plenty of adventures with my old faither. Thought your birthday was the perfect day to tell you…'

Maggie looked at the photograph on the mantelpiece of Granda's Dad, Maggie's Great-Grandfather. He had been in the war like Mrs McNicol, only he had fought in it and won a medal for bravery, having saved the life of his injured commanding sergeant, by carrying him on his own back away from enemy fire. The medal resided in Granda's bedroom in a special box; it was one of his most treasured possessions.

Maggie had been told Great-Granda Ian's stories since before she could remember. He had been very funny and good at magic tricks. He made things out of wood and other bits and pieces people thought were rubbish like bent paperclips. He had known everything there was to know about animals and the outdoors, like where to see just-hatched baby swans without disturbing them, or the names of all the trees and their uses, or how to grow the sweetest, juiciest strawberries. He had worked in the shipyards after the war as a joiner and helped to make them safer places to work through his strong sense of <u>integrity</u> and keen intelligence. His stories reminded Maggie a lot of Granda himself, if truth be told. And so, in that moment, she decided that if her Great-Grandfather and her Granda – people she deeply admired – had believed in the bookcase, then somehow, as crazy as it might seem, she could too.

'Believe me yet?'

His eyebrows were still puckered in an impatient way, but Maggie could also see the creases at his eyes that she associated with the kind of mischief Mum wouldn't usually approve of – that is to say, the very best kind. The kind that might involve 'scientific' experiments where bottles of Cola exploded like volcanoes in the back-garden, or they had extra-extra helpings of Bluebird Café ice-cream, a café and sweet-shop located next to one of Gourock's busy ferry terminals – and Maggie and Granda's favourite place for sweet treats. The ferries were constantly bringing people to and from the Highlands – Gourock and its surrounding towns in Inverclyde lie on the edge of Scotland's Highlands, ideally situated for adventuring North. Maggie and Granda often crossed the River Clyde to visit Dunoon and the

Argyll Hills beyond. Granda had told her lots of old Scottish stories on these trips. If the bookcase was magical – and she didn't quite know what this really meant; would they be able to take journeys with it, or perhaps bring their favourite characters to life? – then this might be the chance to *take part* in some of those old stories!

'You kids nowadays, all hopped-up on your technology, where's your sense of adventure gone, when I was wee…'

'I believe you, I believe you!' Maggie said in a rush, hoping to be spared a rant about the days when a whole <u>tenement-close</u> shared one toilet.

'Course you do,' Granda's whole face at last broke into a wide, crinkly grin, and he took Maggie's small hand in his much larger one, tugging her over to stand before the book-lined shelves.

'Where to then?' he asked, smiling down at his grand-daughter.

'Where? Where *can* we go?' Maggie asked, puzzled again, looking to the bookcase, thinking perhaps she'd see an opening she hadn't noticed before, that maybe they would climb inside. She saw nothing of the sort and looked back at Granda's excited face.

'Anywhere you like, really, as long as it's in these books here,' Granda replied, smile growing at the unconvinced look still clouding Maggie's features. 'I suppose the best place to start is always the very beginning...'

CHAPTER TWO

Granda winked and turned his attention to the books in front of them. He was still a big man, even in his older age when many tend to shrink. That being true, the bookcase was so large that the middle shelves were only to his eye-level; the higher ones towered well over the top of his head. Granda kept a little folding stool beside the bookcase to reach these higher shelves. He squinted at the many spines, his free-hand dancing in mid-air as he tried to locate the precise volume he was looking for.

'Ah, here we are.'

He pulled a massive, ancient-looking book from a high shelf, grunting slightly as the bulk <u>transferred</u> to his hands. He then placed the dusty book in Maggie's arms, the weight of it making her stagger slightly. Granda moved into the middle of the big. square living-room. Bending over with a huff and a slight groan (he had bad knees), he pushed the large coffee table towards the fireplace, away from the centre of the room. He then took the big book from Maggie's arms and laid it open on the slightly-faded fringed rug. With a *hmph* of approval, he checked the page number, patted the book like a pet dog, and straightened back up slowly.

'Ready?' he grinned excitedly, looking suddenly much younger than his old body might suggest. Maggie nodded nervously, wondering what on earth Granda expected to happen next.

'On my count then, lassie, jump–'

'Jump? Onto the book?' Maggie was growing sceptical again. This seemed a bit silly.

'Not onto, *into*, and you've got to mean it, mind, no <u>half-heartedness</u> now.'

Wondering if there was any way you could mean to jump into a book, Maggie readied herself nonetheless. She heard Granda begin to count.

'One…' she was suddenly reminded of the scene in her favourite film where the characters jumped into street-paintings…

'Two…' surely Granda was pulling her leg; this couldn't be serious, could it?

'Three!' Bending her knees and leaping forward, clinging for all she was worth to Granda's hand, she jumped…and they landed in a heap beside each other, the book still lying open innocently on the floor. Maggie looked at it in alarm; she was sure it had <u>deliberately</u> bounced them off!

'That's no good, lass, I told you, you've got to mean it, believe it properly, or the books just won't be interested in sharing their stories with you!'

Maggie wondered how she was supposed to believe any of it, but that books had feelings? This might be a step too far. It was all very silly indeed. And yet, Maggie wanted to believe it, she wanted to go on an adventure, she wanted to see if this was actually real. Could it possibly be real? Repositioning themselves before the book, Maggie concentrated very hard on this desire to know for sure. Granda counted again, and reaching 'THREE!', they both jumped, once more, into the air.

This time, instead of bouncing off the surface of the book as if it were made of rubber, Maggie felt herself glide right into it, like a hole had opened up in the floor. They were sliding into a twisting, dizzying chute, the noise was almost deafening – a roaring wind and a great garble of words all melding together like someone had left the TV, radio (or "wireless", as Granda called it) and iPod on all at once, at full volume. Opening her eyes, Maggie saw the words too, all rushing past in a great swirl of black and white. The only solid, tangible thing she could feel was Granda's hand in hers until, suddenly, quite as abruptly as their ride had begun, their feet found solid, firm ground. They had somehow disappeared right inside the book.

CHAPTER THREE

Maggie looked around, squinting in what was now bright sunlight, a shock to her eyes after the low light in Granda's living room – the weather had been drizzly in Gourock.

'Where are we?' she asked, tightening her grip on Granda's hand slightly, feeling just a little uneasy in the unfamiliar landscape stretching all around them. It was green and heavily wooded. They seemed to be standing on a low hill overlooking a valley thatched with thick stands of woolly trees. There were no roads or buildings in sight, no cars and no people, as far as Maggie could see. Clouds were scudding across the sky, <u>dappling</u> the ground in patches of brilliant light and dark shadow. A cold wind whistled around them, Maggie shivered a little. This was a strange mixture of very, *very* exciting and just a bit scary.

'Still in Scotland,' Granda said. 'Although that's not its name yet.'

Maggie was puzzled by this <u>cryptic</u> sentence.

Granda smiled. 'We're in the land that became Scotland, but we'll be needing to find a different book for that part of the story. Just now we've landed in what the experts at the universities call "Prehistory". This is the time before people wrote things down – before there were any records like birth certificates. There weren't even books at this time, lass; people used to draw and paint on the walls of caves and keep their stories there – or in their heads. Paper hasn't been invented yet; just now people are mostly interested in finding enough food to keep them going through the cold winters. People don't even build 'houses', as we would think of them, anyway...'

'Wow,' Maggie breathed, trying to wrap her head around the last few, magic- and shock-filled minutes. She wasn't hugely successful in this task – it all seemed too impossibly exciting to be real.

Granda watched her expression with interest but made no comment, instead continuing with his explanations: 'This Prehistoric period is actually very important – it's maybe a wee bitty tempting to ignore it because we don't have any written records, which means we don't know what languages people spoke, what names they would have had, what they really looked like or how they sounded. We don't know how they organised their societies – that means, what kinds of rulers they had, like kings or queens or chiefs. We don't know all that much about them, and quite often, their lives leave only the faintest traces, so it's hard to understand them because of all these factors...'

Maggie wondered where, then, they would begin to learn anything!

'...All that is true, but at the same time, it's still really important to understand that they probably weren't all that different from us – they had families and they sang songs and talked about normal, everyday things. Ultimately, they were just people, like you and me.'

That makes things a bit easier, then, Maggie thought, *but still, their world must have been so different from mine.* She was excited to start exploring it.

'These people were our forerunners, <u>pioneers</u> of our own Scotland. They moved into the land after the last Ice Age and had to learn how to live in the often-challenging environment. They had to feed their families and bring in enough food and resources for every season, to make clothing and housing. They had to work everything out and they were clever and skilled at making the tools, clothes and weapons they would have needed to survive. All tough stuff – and they didn't have electricity or anything close to it. In this light, they were really quite remarkable people, Maggie.'

Maggie looked around. She could indeed see no buildings or signs of electricity-pylons (or 'mini-Eifel Towers' as she and Granda called them) of any sort anywhere in the valley. She tried to imagine living with no electric lights or internet, no hot water! "Challenging" Granda had said, "tough"? *Bit of an <u>understatement</u>,* Maggie thought.

'First things first, Maggie,' Granda said, looking out over the landscape. 'This is the time of the Hunter-Gatherers; it's called the "Mesolithic" period, which is a fancy name for the "Middle Stone Age". "Stone Age" because people made most of their tools from stone, by chipping or "knapping" parts off to make points for spears and things like that.'

Maggie mouthed 'Me-so-li-thic' to herself, listening in wonder, committing *'hunter-gatherers living in the Mesolithic or Middle Stone Age'* to memory.

'The Old Stone Age, or Palaeolithic–'

'Palay-what, say that one again, Granda please,' Maggie asked quickly before he could march on with his speech.

'Pa-lay-oh-lith-ic', Granda sounded it out slowly. It was quite a word, Maggie liked the way it rolled off her tongue.

'Palaeolithic,' she repeated a few times.

'That's right, Maggie, so the Palaeolithic, which came before the Mesolithic, was a period when Scotland was mostly empty because there was an Ice Age at the time.'

Maggie thought of the animated films she enjoyed watching with the same title.

'Remember the films?' Granda nodded, reading Maggie's mind. She nodded in turn and Granda went on: 'It was very cold and difficult for people to live during the Ice Age, so Scotland was pretty much uninhabited. The land was stuck under a huge dome of ice. There were some people living on the edges of the ice, probably, coming and going and not staying permanently. The thing is, the ice that covered the land likely destroyed any evidence of people living here in Scotland before then, so we don't know much about that time – it's just one of those things. As I say, ice domes, up to a whole mile thick, covered everything...'

Granda paused, looking out over the landscape. Maggie tried to imagine what that world would have looked like.

'How far is a mile?' she asked. Granda considered this for a moment.

'Well, the Esplanade is just over a mile long,' he answered, referring to the waterfront walk with Greenock's Battery Park at one end and the Container Terminal (Inverclyde's busy sea-port) at the other. Maggie and Granda often walked its length, getting an ice cream (with raspberry sauce) from the Bluebird Café first, then strolling slowly along the Front, through the park to the Esplanade. Occasionally they'd fish over the wall if the weather was fine, or spot visitors off the massive cruise-liners that visited every Summer. 'Let's think, what else…it's the same as…fifteen football pitches, side-by-side – so turn that upright – that's how thick the ice was…'

Maggie was astounded. *Fifteen* football pitches, a mile's worth of ice? She thought of the Saturdays she sometimes spent watching the mighty Greenock Morton playing football, the expanse of the grass they used. Fifteen of those, reaching towards the sky! She could understand why it would have been so difficult to live in that kind of environment.

'Got an idea?' Granda said, smiling at Maggie's dawning comprehension and amazement. 'So, the landscape of Scotland, the hills we love so much, and all the glens pocketed in-between, with the lochs and rivers all winding through – all of it was made by the movement of those big sheets of ice as they began to melt. They gouged out the shapes we have now and sometimes ground down the mountains from much bigger heights–'

'But the hills are massive!' Maggie's wonder only grew the longer Granda spoke. She thought of the trips they'd taken to Glencoe, a glen in Scotland's Highlands, to go hill-walking. Maggie felt so tiny in amongst the mountains, it took a day's hard climb to get to their summits as they stood now!

'Well some were even bigger before the last ice age, and that's how Scotland's landscape was formed, though it took a very, very long time – thousands of years.'

'So why haven't we gone there?' Maggie asked, wondering why they had come to the Middle Stone Age instead.

'Well it's a bit on the cold side apart from anything else,' Granda chuckled, 'And there's not much to see really – it's white and beautiful, but that's about all, so I thought I'd just give you an overview.'

Maggie realised she did agree; she was chilly enough standing here and shivered a little at the thought of all that ice.

'It's thought that, at best guess, there were people living in Scotland – at least for some of the year – up to fourteen thousand years ago!' Granda said.

Maggie couldn't quite get her head around such an amount of time.

'But here we are in the Mesolithic, which in Scotland happened around about eight thousand years ago…' Granda nodded, pleased with the look of amazement upon Maggie's face once more.

That was still a really, really long time ago, she thought. *This **is** a really long time ago*; she corrected herself, head spinning a little. She wondered if it was all just a thrilling dream and gave herself a nip in the crook of her arm to be sure. She didn't wake up at home in bed – it all really seemed to be happening!

'Right,' Granda began again, 'It'll be easier if we *see* what this time was all about, rather than listening to me natter on: let's go this way…'

They set off in the direction Granda was
pointing, along the ridge of the hill. Maggie could
see the sea from up here, over on her left. The
waves crashed and rolled, white foam ridging a
narrow strip of sandy shore. There were jagged
rocks just behind this thin line of sand, the water
rolling right up into them. Maggie knew there
would be great rock-pools down there, suddenly
wishing she had her wee red net with her.

Maggie and Granda often went exploring
the rock-pools down at Lunderston Bay or Fairlie;
it was one of Maggie's favourite things to do,
finding limpets, cockles and mussels. Once or
twice they had even come across some star-fish or
a sea urchin. She liked finding bits of sea-glass
and wondering what they had once been part of –
someone's message-in-a-bottle perhaps? She

always longed to find a message-in-a-bottle in-tact and write back to whoever had sent it.

The ground was rocky up on the ridge and Maggie picked her way carefully along while lost in her thoughts. The wind was still whistling around them. It had been very late in the Spring-time at home, even though it was raining (it often rained in Gourock), and Maggie was only wearing a t-shirt and jeans. She was beginning to get cold.

'Ah! See the smoke? Granda pointed ahead. Maggie could see the thin pillar of smoke winding its way into the air on the other side of a dense forest. 'We're headed in the right direction, that'll be a home-camp, I should think…'

Maggie looked at Granda with a thrill of excitement and – she had to admit – fear. Where there was smoke, there were people – and where there were people there would <u>undoubtedly</u> be questions about how, exactly, Maggie and Granda had appeared, *literally*, from thin air...

CHAPTER FOUR

They walked along side-by-side and Granda began once more with his explaining:

'Hunter-gatherers do what their name suggests. This time was even before farming was developed, Maggie, so people weren't growing food to eat – they were *gathering* wild foods – plants and fruits, seafood and the like, and *hunting* bigger animals and fishing. They didn't build 'houses' as we think of them, or anything like that; they often made camps and moved around the country to get their hands on the best food and materials to make tools and weapons to hunt and protect themselves. The land looked quite different– '

Granda gestured widely at the landscape around them. ' –the rivers were bigger in Prehistory, so this made the place more of a set of big islands. A lot of people's time would have been spent 'island-hopping' to find the best resources from different parts of the country. They were likely great sailors, using boats made from animal hides and wood called 'curraghs' or 'coracles'. They could move on the water quickly and easily, using up a lot less energy than walking everywhere, since the land would have been very wild. A great forest covered a huge chunk of Scotland around this time, full of dangerous animals – bears, wild-cats, wolves and the like.'

Maggie looked quickly around them, eyes peeled for any signs of bears or wolves following or getting ready to pounce. She didn't see any, thankfully, but her excitement was now tinged with a little more alertness, a deeper edge of fear.

She tried to imagine the world Granda was describing – which wasn't too difficult since she was looking at it. But her head still seemed to be in competition with itself, between accepting what she was seeing to be real and the impossibility of being *inside* a book.

She had always believed in magic, in fairies and other unseen, but nonetheless-present creatures like brownies and 'wee folk'. She couldn't have grown up listening to Scotland's many wonderful folk- and fairy-tales from Granda and not believed in some way. And yet, she was still having a hard time believing in the bookcase. It was just too *cool* not to question. Adding dangerous wild animals to the mix was another level of excitement. She shivered slightly, though not just from cold this time.

'And, eh, do we have to worry about the bears and wild-cats and wolves?' she asked, hoping she sounded casual and unaffected. She wasn't *scared*, she just thought it would be sensible to know if she'd need to run away from a massive, hungry bear at any point in the near-future.

'Hmmmm...' Granda considered this question, pinching the skin beneath his chin with two fingers, as he did when he was thinking. He looked as if he'd never considered the possibility Maggie had pointed out, which made Maggie's worry increase, just a little. '...nah, I shouldn't think there's much to worry about here – if the Mesolithic people have a camp, it's likely a fairly safe area. We'll keep our eyes peeled anyway, eh?' Granda winked at Maggie. 'Don't worry Mags, your old Granda still has a few tricks up his sleeve, you're safe with me. Well, fairly safe...'

His eyes were crinkling in his mischievous way and Maggie felt better. Granda did always look after her, even when they went on crazy adventures – even on this craziest adventure of all, that wouldn't change.

'Well now, here they are! See over there?' Granda pointed. Maggie suddenly noticed too, that there was a small group of people making their way down to the sea-shore from the general direction of the smoke. They had large, woven bowls in their arms and were chattering amongst themselves in a language Maggie couldn't understand. In fact, it sounded like no language she had ever heard before. It was fascinating.

A small number of children who looked to be around Maggie's age came hurtling into view, calling and laughing, chasing each other around. They looked tough and strong, their legs launching them high into the air as they leapt from boulder to boulder towards the sandy shore.

'I wonder what they're saying...' Maggie thought aloud.

'Oh here, lass, I forgot–' Granda reached into the pocket of his navy-blue corduroy trousers and extracted what looked like his regular TV remote from home. Maggie's brow creased in confusion, as she wondered what exactly was coming next.

'I told you I had some tricks up my sleeve, well I should have said, in my pocket!' Granda pointed the remote at the group of people. He pressed a sequence of numbers into it and somehow, like a radio being tuned-in with its signal coming and going, the words drifting over from the group began to make sense to Maggie's ears. She could understand what they were saying, even though it still wasn't English she was hearing. It was the strangest feeling ever.

'Better?' Granda said with a big grin.

'Weird.' Maggie shook her head in amazement and Granda laughed his deep, rumbly laugh.

'Thought it was just a regular doo-dah, did you?' (this was the word Granda always used for the TV remote).

Maggie grinned up at him. 'Just like I thought it was just a regular bookcase!'

They laughed together for a few moments, then turned their attention back to the people in the distance.

Maggie could hear snatches of conversation carrying over on the wind. The people were talking about the weather and gathering enough food for the cold coming in. The sea would be getting stormy and destructive soon, they were saying; they would have to time their journeys to the Outer Islands well to avoid the storms. As Maggie listened, she realised she could recognise some of the sounds they were making; letter combinations like 'sh' and 'ch' were frequent. With his usual unnerving, almost telepathic skill, Granda seemed to read her mind.

'Some of the sounds are familiar to you Maggie, because they're 'anatomically-modern' people, do you know what that means?'

She shook her head, no, but made a guess by saying, 'Anatomically, like their bodies?'

'Got it in one,' Granda smiled. 'Their bodies, or 'anatomy', are the same as ours in terms of how they're made up, they all have internal organs – lungs and kidneys and brains the same rough size to ours. That means that they make speech sounds in the same way we do – some of the sounds must be the same as English or any other modern language, because humans can only make so many different sounds with their speech organs,' he paused at Maggie's slightly puzzled look and added, 'that's the tongue and voice-box and all that stuff in your throat and mouth' nodding when he saw that Maggie understood. 'So, different languages combine these different sounds, some languages use sounds that others don't, but what we're hearing here is an <u>ancestor</u> of all the languages in our own, modern world.'

Maggie liked languages, she had immensely enjoyed listening to the rapid Spanish of the locals when she, Mum, Dad and Granda had visited Mallorca on holiday the previous year. She had wished that she could understand and speak the language too. Granda had even bought a Spanish-language course when Maggie had told him this, so that they could learn together and be able to pick up a bit more the next time they had a holiday in Spain.

'Can we get closer?' Maggie asked, while at the same time wondering if this was a good idea, she still didn't know how they would explain their presence in the Mesolithic if they were seen.

'Aye, just a second, let me see, what's the combination again...' Granda peered down at the remote, perching his glasses on his nose, brow furrowing in concentration.

'Was it 8512?' he murmured to himself, typing in the number. Maggie gasped aloud, astonished to feel that a heavy, fur cape had <u>materialised</u> around her own shoulders. She frowned in wonder at the innocent-looking remote and wondered just what else it could do. She couldn't wait to find out! In a way, she was almost *annoyed* at it, (which was very silly, of course but still); it had never done anything close to interesting at home. Not one hint of its real powers had she ever seen! The same went for the bookcase, and she just thanked her lucky stars that Granda thought that ten was the right age to learn about it all – this was too much fun not to be in on!

Granda was continuing to have some difficulty with the remote.

'Nope that's not right, looks good on you though, lassie, that'll keep you a bit warmer too...might get myself one now that I've done that.'

He began typing the numbers in again, and Maggie stood on tip-toe, placing her hands on his forearm to bring the remote closer to her eye-level so that she could see the marvellous contraption in action. Another cape appeared around Granda's shoulders.

'Och aye, that's better,' he shrugged the cape into a more comfortable position, still scrutinising the remote. Maggie stepped back to admire him in his cape, smiling.

'Was it 9549?' he said to himself and tried this number. Maggie cried aloud as Granda disappeared completely from her side.

'Granda! Where have you gone?' panic was rising like cold water in Maggie's chest – what if she got stuck here alone? Granda hadn't told her how to get out of the book!

'I'm here, lass, still here, right beside you.'

She suddenly felt the reassuring weight of Granda's large hand on her shoulder, though her heart was still hammering unpleasantly.

'Look down–' Granda's weirdly disembodied voice said. Maggie looked down, shock jumping through her arms and legs once more: her own body had disappeared too! Maggie raised her hand in front of her face. It was definitely there: she could feel it, could feel the air moving against her face as she waved her arm vigorously, but there was absolutely nothing to be seen. The sensation was very odd.

'I've made us invisible Maggie, don't want to upset the folks down there by popping up so unexpectedly – or get ourselves into bother. Neat wee trick eh?' he said with a chuckle, though of course, Maggie couldn't see his smile. 'Right, take my hand and hold tight so we don't get separated. If we do get separated don't panic – just make an ocarina with your hands and do the wood pigeon call I showed you last week at Cornalees. Have a practice now.'

Granda was excellent at bird calls. He had taught Maggie how to imitate the low, cooing call of the wood pigeon by blowing into her hands just last week when they went for a walk in the woods at Cornalees, a nature reserve near Gourock. Granda called this an "ocarina" or hand-whistle and had told Maggie that it was an ancient way of making music. Remembering the technique, Maggie made a chamber with her two small hands. Lining up her thumbs, she placed her lips to the knuckles and blew gently, creating the distinctive throaty bird call. She tried to remember the rhythm as accurately as possible.

'Aye very good, lass, you always did pick things up fast,' Granda ruffled Maggie's already unruly curly hair, though his invisible state meant that he clapped her rather hard, misjudging her height slightly. 'Oops, sorry lassie!' Granda guffawed as Maggie stumbled.

'Gran-daaa!' Maggie half-grumbled, half-laughed, straightening back up and giving Granda a playful nudge in return.

'C'mon then, let's get going,' Granda found Maggie's hand and took it securely once more. They began to pick their way down to the shore.

'Mind keep nice and quiet now,' Granda whispered as they drew closer to the people on the beach.

Maggie could now see that they were exploring the rock pools, just like she did with her wee red net. They all wore surprisingly well-fitting clothes, made from furs and other animal skins. Maggie had imagined they'd be rough or lacking in skill in some way – the clothes were the complete opposite. They fitted each person well, close to their bodies, without, it would seem, hampering their movements in any way. Both the men and women had long hair, though the males all had it cut shorter, brushing their shoulders. The women's hair, however, skimmed the bases of their backs in long, thick plaits or flew freely on the brisk sea-breeze. They all had white shells corded into their hair too, framing their faces attractively, and many wore strings of what looked like teeth around their necks and wrists. They all seemed strong and well-built, layers of clothing and capes adding bulk.

The men and women had small tools in their hands and were balancing the large woven bowls on their hips. They were using the tools to dig shellfish from the sand, some were prying small <u>crustaceans</u> swiftly from the rocky sides of the pools, then depositing them in the quickly-filling bowls. It was a proper team effort, with everyone working efficiently side-by-side. Even the children were helping, climbing to pools further up in the rocky boulders with cat-like agility. Every now and again Maggie could hear a small sucking sound as the limpets parted company with the rocks.

A little way apart from the group at the pools, were a second small cluster of men, women and children, to whom the full bowls were being brought. They were using a slightly differently-shaped tool to remove the shells from the limpets and mussels. The shells were then being thrown onto a rapidly-growing pile.

'See their tools? The ones they're digging with are called 'mattocks', probably made from bits of antler. And see the pile?' Granda's voice whispered from beside Maggie. 'That's what's called a 'midden' or rubbish heap. There isn't much material evidence – leftovers, if you like – for this part of Prehistory, because it was so long ago. We rely on the remains of these kinds of piles to give information about the period – how people lived and what they ate and so on.'

'Mum calls my bedroom a midden sometimes,' Maggie frowned and Granda chuckled.

'Well you'll need to remember to keep it a bit tidier then...!'

Maggie looked at the pile and the <u>industrious</u> workers. It took a lot of work to make a midden. A wide grin spread across her face as she thought that she'd need to tell her Mum this the next time she scolded Maggie about the state of her room.

CHAPTER FIVE

They watched the group for a while until they started gathering their tools and baskets of food together and calling the children over. Maggie felt Granda guiding her along to follow in their wake. They walked a short way, skirting the edge of the thick, dark forest they'd seen from the ridge, before entering a small camp, hidden from view by the trees. It was set in a shallow hollow, protected from the brisk sea-wind by another high ridge. The houses didn't look all that hard-wearing to Maggie. They were really just tents; small, domed structures with wooden pegs holding animal skins taut over wooden frames. There was a large fire in the centre of the camp and people milling around, some tending to the fire, carefully turning rounded parcels sitting in pits in its centre. The air was filled with the delicious smell of roasting hazelnuts – *that must be what's in the parcels*, Maggie thought. Her tummy gave a gurgle, the smell made her think of Christmas shopping in Glasgow.

Maggie looked around the camp, taking in more details of its layout and contents. There was a wooden frame standing in a sheltered corner, upon which leaned a number of lethal-looking spears and harpoons, with stone points tied onto wooden handles. A bundle of arrows was laid across two of the timbers at the top-most point of the A-framed structure. A similar wooden construction had large animal skins draped over it, looking like they were being dried-out before being used to make clothes or tent-skins. In a neat line between the tents, a row of upturned boats lay. They were similar in many ways to the tents – in fact Maggie had mistaken them for tents at first glance. They were a similar, rounded shape; wooden frames with an animal skin drawn tightly over them.

'Curraghs,' Granda whispered. 'Those boats, they're the curraghs I was talking about. Probably made with deer skins.'

Next, Granda tugged Maggie towards a large area set back between two of the tents. Here a man and a woman were working on some new tools. The man was kneeling before a large, flat stone. He was working on a tool similar to the ones being used to pry the sea-food from the rocks. Using a large stone to strike a smaller one, he split it into smaller chunks. The woman was using what looked to Maggie like the tine of an antler to chip smaller pieces off the hunks the man had made. Tiny chips were flying from it, landing in a spray around the work-area. Slowly the tool became neater and sharper, the more she chipped away and shaped it. The workers' touch was practised and swift; they obviously knew what they were doing.

A boy, maybe a year or two older than Maggie sat behind the man and woman, watching them carefully. Now and again, the man motioned to the boy, demonstrating exactly what he was doing with his hands. The boy must have been learning to work the stone too.

The woman was now bending over a tiny piece of stone, so small in fact, that Maggie nearly couldn't see it at all. From what she could see, it looked like a triangular shape, but Maggie would have to ask Granda exactly what kind of tool could be useful at such a small size. There was a small pile of finished points beside her, and Maggie realised they might be points for arrows, or something along those lines.

Maggie's attention was caught by a movement behind the stone-workers, from the dark line of the trees. For a second she thought with a thrill of fear that it could be an animal, ready to pounce from the cover of the trees. It turned out to be a large man carrying a long spear, the end of which was sharpened to a deadly point. He was walking slowly and deliberately back and forth, along the length of the camp that was exposed to the trees. He was a guard, she understood, making sure that there were *no* surprise animal attacks. She thought this was a sensible precaution and wondered once more at the lifestyle these people led, the dangers they faced on a regular basis. *It must have been a hard life.*

A short time later, Maggie felt Granda squeeze her hand. He began pulling her back the way they had come, leaving the Mesolithic hunters to their tasks and their lives. They walked in silence until they were a distance from the camp and the incline to the ridge had evened a little. Reaching roughly the same point they had arrived, Maggie watched Granda re-materialise before her eyes, stowing the remote back in his pocket.

'The thing to remember, Mags is that, like I said, no one wrote anything down at this time, so we don't really know what it was actually like. Everything we do know is 'reconstructed'. The clever folk at the universities – people called Archaeologists – dig in the ground to find things Prehistoric people left behind–'

'Like Indiana Jones?' Maggie asked thinking of one of Granda's favourite film series. Maggie liked them quite a lot too. Indiana was an Archaeologist, and he was constantly adventuring. Maggie thought she might like to be one when she grew up.

'Like that, yeah, only Indiana Jones has a bit more adventure than most Archaeologists I'm sure,' Granda said, smiling. Maggie was a little disappointed, if truth be told.

'Anyway, these Archaeologists find bits of tools, rubbish heaps and things like that and fill in the rest of the details with what are called _interpretations_. That basically means that we use what we do know about the period – the bits and pieces of tools and things – and reconstruct, or "build up a picture of" what the past could have been like. We can see the people here, what they're doing and how they're doing it but we don't know for definite if that's what really went on. This book and everything in it is only one person's *idea* of what this time was like.'

Maggie nodded slowly, digesting everything Granda had just said. It all made sense; things that happened so long ago couldn't really be expected to leave a lot of evidence behind.

'Did you see how the man and woman were making that tool – remember I mentioned – it's called "knapping", chipping wee bits off to make the right shape and size. It's quite a skill, and the wee bits flying in all directions can be dangerous, especially for the eyes. They knew what they were doing though; did you see how fast they were?' Granda asked and Maggie nodded.

'Was that a bit of antler she was using?' she asked.

'Looked like it didn't it? Similar to the mattocks they were using on the beach. The big stone the man was using was called a 'cobble'. That gave him the rough size he wanted for the tool, then the shape was fine-tuned with the antler.'

'And what was the woman making? It was tiny! Was it a point for an arrow?' Maggie asked.

'Aye probably lass, that's a good shout,' Granda nodded in agreement. 'An arrow-point or maybe a small spear-point. They needed weapons like that for hunting wild animals. They also made harpoons with those bits of bone, to catch bigger fish too. The stone points are called *microliths*, Maggie' Granda sounded out the word slowly. 'The Mesolithic is kind of defined by microliths –

they're one of the most common finds from the period. "Micro" because they're so small and "lith" meaning "stone".'

Maggie thought that made perfect sense.

'The wee bits that were flying about from the knapping create what are called 'scatter sites' – literally just a scattering of wee bits of stone that all have a similar shape. These scatters tell Archaeologists that these were places where tools were made. Scatter sites, alongside middens, are the most common sites for the Scottish Mesolithic, and even these don't often survive and are hard to find most of the time. Think about the tents – they would have been easy to carry around and set up elsewhere, but they haven't left much of a trace to find thousands of years later.'

Maggie took it all in as Granda spoke; it was dawning on her just how difficult it was to understand exactly how the past would have looked and how the people would have lived. Archaeologists were obviously very smart and very patient!

'In terms of the community, one idea is that people lived in smaller groups most of the time, but came together in a bigger camp like this one to prepare for the winter.'

'But there were only about twenty people there – that's a bigger group?' Maggie was surprised.

'That's right, lass, the communities would have been much smaller in Prehistory, and people wouldn't have lived all that long, maybe only to about forty or fifty years of age at the very, very oldest. They didn't have healthcare like we do, or even any real medicines. They were hunting big animals and crossing rough seas, making and using tools without safety equipment, maybe even going without food now and again if they couldn't gather enough. It was likely a hard, dangerous life.'

Maggie was a little sad for the Mesolithic people; they really had it quite tough. They had seemed to be managing though. It was amazing how well they fared, really, without any modern tools, no electricity or internet or anything! They had to make everything they needed themselves; had to build fires to keep warm and cook, boats to fish, they even had to make tools to make other tools! *How hard it must have been*, Maggie thought to herself.

'Just off the coast, out that way–' Granda pointed towards the sea, in a north-westerly direction. 'is the island of Rùm. There's a place called Kinloch there, which is a site with dates as early as 6600 BC. People went to get 'bloodstone', which they then used to make tools – remember I was saying about 'island-hopping'? That man's cobble was probably a bloodstone from Rùm.'

Maggie looked out over the rough, unforgiving sea. She could imagine how hard the journey to Rùm would be – and sailing, Granda had said, was *easier* than any other way of travelling! She tried unsuccessfully to suppress a shiver, in spite of the heavy cape she was still wearing.

'The sea looks scary to us, and even in our time you really need to know what you're doing out on the water – and we have all sorts of tools and equipment for finding our way, compasses and sonar and things like that. The Prehistoric people relied on stories and landmarks and the position of the sun in the sky. They were skilled sailors and used all the Hebridean Islands at different times of the year for different resources. Those hazelnuts we smelled could have come from the island of Colonsay. There were no squirrels on Colonsay for the people to compete with, so there were lots and lots of hazelnuts to be found there.'

Maggie thought some more about sailing versus walking. She thought of the hillwalking she'd done with Mum, Dad and Granda. Carrying a backpack was hard work. Imagine if you were carrying all your belongings – and tools made from stone no less! It would have taken so much time and energy on the rough terrain she had seen, with no roads or real paths or anything. If the people could sail around, it would have been easier to carry equipment and the foods they'd gathered. Even in Maggie's own time, Scotland had so many lochs and rivers. Maggie and her family lived on a what she thought of as a huge river, the Clyde, and lots of boats sailed up and down it every day. The water must really have provided an easy, quick way to move around in the past. The area they were visiting today must have been a good place to live and travel around, with the big islands full of food nearby, like Granda had said.

Maggie's thoughts were interrupted as Granda said, 'Right let's fast-forward a bit, see what else we can find out...'

CHAPTER SIX

Taking out his remote once more, Granda pressed the TV Guide button and a small, flickering window suddenly appeared in front of them. Maggie walked around the window, <u>suspended</u> as it was, in mid-air. She was amazed once more, passing her hand through the hologram. It wasn't solid, but it wasn't completely without substance either; her hand tingled pleasantly with a sensation like mild pins and needles. The window looked like the Contents Page of a book and Maggie understood as Granda aimed the remote at the page he was looking for.

'Hand Maggie, quick now–'

She ran over and took Granda's outstretched hand as he pressed the 'Enter' button in the centre of the remote. With a great lurch, the ground beneath their feet began rolling slowly like a treadmill, rumbling like thunder as it went. Maggie and Granda began to run as the ground picked up speed, rippling and changing colour rapidly. A great wind ruffled Maggie's hair as they were hurtled through the book's pages, and it was all Maggie could do to keep upright.

Just as she thought she was going to fall, everything came to an abrupt halt once more, the same way it had when they had jumped into the book to begin with. She wobbled with the sudden ceasing of forward-momentum, then fell forward, landing hard on her hands and knees. Granda had managed to remain upright, obviously a bit more used to the quick-dash and sudden stops of the books. He helped Maggie to her feet, dusting her off and smiling.

'You'll get used to it, don't worry.'

Maggie sighed a little at the slight green smudges on the knees of her jeans. Mum would be annoyed at more grass stains – Maggie was always coming home with dirty clothes from her tree-climbing, commando-make-believing, den-building and general love of the outdoors. It was a good thing she hadn't put on her newer jeans, then Mum *really* wouldn't have been happy! As it was, the ones she was wearing were getting a little short on Maggie anyway, and still bore the marks of one of she and Granda's 'projects' from last week.

They had been building a model sailing ship and had decided it needed a coat of paint.

The bright blue stains hadn't come out in the wash; there were still two perfect fingerprints on the left-hand pocket. Maggie thought they looked kind of cool, if truth be told. Mum did not.

The ship had actually sailed though, so it had been worth it. They'd taken it to Cove's Reservoir for its maiden voyage and it had floated like a dream...for a few seconds. Then a swift wind had keeled it over on one side and they'd had to fish it out with a long stick and some help (or hindrance as was more accurately the case), from Wally the Westie. Granda thought he knew what the ship's problem was, and it was sitting in the workshop awaiting repairs before a second sailing could be undertaken.

Maggie thought about her Mum's aversion to dirt. She grinned as she remembered Granda getting-at Mum for getting-at Maggie's muddy trainers, one wet Sunday.

'You were the exact same at that age Debbie-Dorah! Worse even! Leave Mags be, she's just exploring the world...' he'd said with a wave of his large hand, using the nickname he always did for Mum.

Mum couldn't hide her own smile at his words and had given Maggie a wink. As much as she wished Maggie could be tidier and come home cleaner, her Mum really was good fun to be around. Mum could climb higher trees than Dad, Maggie had seen it for herself! And it was all Granda's influence – he had never believed in putting children in boxes or wrapping them in cotton wool. Maggie was as encouraged to play with dolls as she was to climb trees and play football – and Maggie's Mum had been raised this way too. But now, something occurred to Maggie – did her Mum know about the bookcase? Had she been keeping it a secret too? Had she gone on wonderful journeys like this one with Granda?

'Earth calling Maggie-Moo...' Granda said, waving at her. She had been lost in her head but now smiled at Granda, ready for the next part of their adventure and ready to find out what exactly Mum knew when they returned home. For now, she took in their new surroundings. They were standing in a green glen, surrounded by thickly-wooded hills. The sun was beating down strongly; the capes had disappeared from their shoulders, but there was little need for them now anyway.

Even with the thick covering of trees on the slopes, there were less here than there had been in the Mesolithic landscape, Maggie thought. The sun was warmer now too – *it must be summer here,* she mused. Both Maggie and Granda were still panting a little, Maggie felt the beginnings of a stitch in her side. She hadn't been quite prepared for their sprint through the pages of the book.

Granda massaged his own chest, breathing hard. 'You were far away there, lass, still adjusting to the excitement, are you?'

Maggie nodded.

'I'm a bit out of puff,' Granda continued. 'It's been a while.'

Maggie wondered if 'a while' had been since her Mum had been a ten-year-old.

'Still we're here now!' Granda said.

'And where is 'here' exactly, Granda?' Maggie asked, distracted for now by the adventure at hand. She looked around the grassy field in which they stood.

'This here is a place called Kilmartin Glen, lassie, and we're now in the Neolithic era, that's the 'New Stone Age', which happened in Scotland around about 4000-2000 BC.'

Another new word! Maggie reminded herself that the order was: Palaeolithic ("Old Stone Age"); Mesolithic "Middle Stone Age"; and now Neolithic ("New Stone Age"), noticing that the "m" in "Mesolithic" and "Middle" matched, as did the "n" in "Neolithic" and "New". This would be handy for remembering.

Granda had paused, watching Maggie thinking through the new information. When she looked at him to continue he followed her lead:

'The Scottish Neolithic is defined by the beginnings of farming – the Neolithic people were the first farmers. We're about 3000 years or so further on from the Mesolithic where we started out...'

Three thousands years in a few seconds of running! Maggie thought, feeling better about being out-of-breath. *Not many people could say they'd done that!* She smiled to herself, enjoying her birthday more than she ever thought possible.

Granda was still talking '...Another thing, though, like not knowing much in the way of proper details about Prehistory, is that we don't have precise dates for it either. People didn't go to bed as Mesolithic Hunter-Gatherers and wake up as Neolithic farmers. It would have taken a long time for these things to develop and change, and it wouldn't have happened all-at-once all over Scotland. It would have happened in different places at different times and at different speeds.'

Maggie did her best to absorb all of this information. History was turning out to be quite a complicated affair...

'There's a big debate about how the Neolithic and the move to farming came about,' Granda went on. 'Some people think that a whole new set of people came in from other countries in Europe, especially Northern France, and brought their farming lifestyles with them. Others think that the farming *ideas* came from other places and the Scottish Mesolithic people took them up slowly, replacing their old ways with farming after a long transition. We know that there were some climate changes around the time of the change-over that made some of the Mesolithic resources unreliable – rising sea-levels and such like. People would have *had* to look elsewhere for food sources.'

Maggie's head was beginning to spin again. This really was a lot to take in.

'What do you think, Granda? How do you think the change happened?' she asked, because Granda always worked things out in a way that made sense to her.

'Well, lass, I think it was probably a mix of all of those things – the climate changed so people needed new ways of finding food, new ideas came in with new people and slowly the indigenous – that's the people who were living here already, the 'native' people – adopted farming as their way of life. Maybe it's a bit simplistic, but it's logical to me and logical enough for our purposes here today anyway.'

'That seems sensible to me too,' Maggie agreed.

Granda stood catching his breath for a few moments, enjoying the sun on his face before ploughing on with his explanation.

'So, by the Neolithic period, people were beginning to farm. They were clearing forests to make way for fields so they could grow crops. Pottery appeared for the first time, probably brought in like farming from Northern France. They had started settling in one place for longer periods of time, started building more substantial structures. Their belief systems were developing with these new farming habits too, at least, the beliefs were leaving more of a mark than they ever had before.'

'Granda, what's a belief system?' Maggie asked, puzzled by this term and what Granda had meant by them "leaving a mark".

'Well, it's like religion – the things people believe and the…the sort-of *rules* they live by according to those beliefs. Like, think about how we go to Mass every Sunday, or Muslims saying their prayers five times a day, facing in the direction of Mecca–'

'Or like Jews and <u>Passover</u>? Or Hindus and <u>Diwali</u>?' Maggie had cottoned-on, remembering the lessons she'd had at school about other world religions.

'Exactly, clever-cookie, you've got the idea – in the Neolithic, people lived by belief systems which were probably closely-linked to nature and the cycle of the seasons, since those cycles affected what they grew and when. They might praise the moon because its monthly phases and positions in the sky meant that there were certain times of the year best for harvesting their crops. Or they worshipped the sun because fine weather helped crops to grow, that sort of thing.'

Maggie nodded along with Granda's explanations, thinking about life in the Neolithic, about living from the land.

'It's hard to know exactly what they believed and how they worshipped, just like we don't have much detail for any other part of Prehistoric life. We do know that by the Neolithic period they were building structures that Archaeologists think were part of religious-type ceremonies and rituals. That's why we've come to Kilmartin. Of course, that's not its name at the moment – not sure what they call it here in the Neolithic...' Granda continued and looked around serenely, as if this were the most normal thing in the world; to be standing in a field in the Neolithic period, wondering what the locals called that field. Maggie was enjoying herself immensely, this was all still pretty bizarre, but what an adventure!

Looking around properly now, she could see huge stones protruding from the otherwise flat expanse of the green field – some of these 'bigger structures' that Granda was on about, she understood. They seemed randomly-placed at first, but Maggie took a second to notice that they made a kind of X shape. There were two sets of double stones, standing side-by-side, with maybe ten Maggie-sized paces between them. These two sets were in turn a good fifty or more paces away from each other. In the middle of the rough, narrow rectangle these made, there was a fifth stone, this one the biggest of all.

Granda followed Maggie's line of sight and said, 'These are the Nether Largie Standing Stones, Maggie – part of those bigger, ritual monuments and belief-systems I've been talking about. If the Mesolithic was defined by 'microliths' – tiny pieces of worked-stone, then the Neolithic is marked by *megaliths* – massive monuments made of stone, just like these ones. No one's really sure what their purpose was – hopefully we'll manage to find out while we're here!'

Maggie took in the shape of the stones. As she was learning to do at school, she thought of the metre-sticks they had for measuring. These stones were roughly two and a half metre-sticks in height, she estimated, towering over she and Granda. Their edges were fairly straight, each roughly rectangular, but some with an angle to their tops. Maggie looked again at each in turn and noticed a pattern emerging. The four 'corner stones' were angled slightly towards each other on top. The big, centre stone was flat-topped. Its surfaces were pock-marked, but Maggie couldn't see from this distance exactly what the markings were.

'Let's talk a bit more about belief systems before we try and see them first-hand,' Granda said. 'Now one of the things we have a bit of evidence for, is the way people in Prehistory treated their loved ones who had died. In our time, we have a funeral and people are usually laid to rest in coffins in the ground, or cremated and kept in urns or scattered.'

Maggie thought this was a bit of a morbid topic, but listened carefully nonetheless.

'In the Neolithic, people seem to have built *chambered tombs* or *cairns*, especially in the Northern and Western Isles. Although there was a lot of 'regional diversity', Maggie, which means that people in different places did things a bit differently. We don't have to worry too much about the details of that for now, though – we just want a rough idea' he winked at Maggie. 'Just know that they were 'chambered' because the tombs formed a chamber, made from stone or wood, where the bodies were put. There are chambered tombs and cairns all over Kilmartin, or there *will* be – in our time they're called the 'linear cemetery', because they've found four or five chambered cairns in a line, (that's the 'linear' part), right up the length of the glen.'

He held a hand over his eyes to shade them from the sun before turning Maggie on the spot and pointing. 'Ah! Do you see that bright spot away in the distance? That's one of them! Maybe Nether Largie South, as it's known in our time.'

Maggie could see the massive mound in the distance and shivered a little. People were *buried* there. She wanted to know more, in spite of herself. 'So, people are put there when they die?' she asked.

'Yes, Maggie – in the Neolithic when people died, Archaeologists think that they were *excarnated*. What that means is that they would be put out in the open air, usually on raised platforms so that big animals couldn't get at them. The wind, rain and birds would clean the bodies until only the bones were left...'

Maggie couldn't help but feel a bit queasy picturing this sight.

'...some of these tombs, called "passage graves", had channels leading to different chambers inside them. After the excarnation bit, there might have been a special ceremony when the clean bones were *interred* into the chambers. That means 'laid to rest',' he added, seeing Maggie open her mouth to ask. 'The bones were sometimes separated into different compartments inside, for instance, all the leg bones in one place, all the skulls in another and so on.'

Maggie contemplated this information. It was certainly strange to her, but it had obviously made sense to the Neoliths. In some way, Maggie could understand that a grave of this kind meant that everyone sort of, 'became one' after they died; a mass of ancestors. It was perhaps a nice thought, really, being all mixed up with the people you loved forever.

'Look, watch, this is quite something–' Granda broke into her thoughts.

He took the remote and pointed it at nothing in particular. He keyed in some numbers and a hologram appeared in the air in front of them, similar to the Contents Page from earlier. This time they were looking at a large, green mound. There was a narrow opening in the middle of the front of the mound.

'This here is a wee bit later in date than other chambered tombs here – it's one of the "passage graves" I mentioned, from a place called Maes Howe on Orkney. There's a whole lot of Neolithic-era stuff up there, would be good to show you it all, but there's just not enough time!

We could take a trip in the summer holidays, maybe, see all the building remains first-hand...'

Maggie nodded <u>enthusiastically</u> at this suggestion while Granda continued. 'For now, look here – the opening you see in the front of the tomb was made to line-up with the sun at the Winter Solstice each year. A 'solstice' is the middle-point of the summer or winter. In winter, the solstice is the shortest day, when the sun is lowest in the sky. The corridor inside the passage-grave at Maes Howe would have been flooded with light as the sun set at that point in the year. You can imagine that that would have been an impressive sight.'

Maggie could indeed imagine this and was also amazed that the Neolithic people could make something so specifically to line up with the sun's position in the sky at a single point in each year. Granda pressed the fast-forward button and a miniature sun rose at double-speed over the tomb. As it reached the lowest, most western point of the hologram sky, a beam of light shone into the narrow corridor. Maggie tried to picture what it would have looked like from inside, thinking of all the separated piles of bones. She could feel goosebumps rising on her arms and a prickle ran across her nose.

'People who were quite new to farming, who relied on the sun to grow their crops, would obviously respect it, worship it even, and would worry that it might suddenly stop shining. They would have been hoping that the sun would come back again, even when the days were coldest and shortest. A structure like Maes Howe might have allowed them to mark the hardest part of the winter and know that summer would soon be coming back. It might also have acted as a gift, or an offering to the sun-god, asking them to return for another summer.'

Maggie watched as the hologram disappeared, lost in thought.

'It would be an important time of the year then, a bit like Christmas to us?' she asked.

'Exactly, Maggie, and there was probably a celebration at the Summer Solstice too, come to think of it – the longest day of the year, when the sun would be highest in the sky. It might be a thanksgiving-type of thing...' Granda trailed off, eyes set on a far-off spot, deep in thoughts of his own.

'Now, I wonder...' he murmured to himself, raising a hand to shield his eyes again and peering into the distance. Maggie wanted to investigate the huge stones in front of them. While Granda looked around, still muttering to himself, she wandered from his side. She'd go and see what the marks on the centre stone were. As she stepped into the "box" made by the stones, a cold, swift wind suddenly picked-up, lifting Maggie's hair from her neck and raising more goosebumps all over her arms.

'Maggie! Come back over here!' Granda's voice was sharp, a little panicked.

Maggie hurried away from the stones, back to Granda's side.

'Was that me? That made the wind come like that?' she asked, eyes wide with shock.

'I'm not sure, Maggie, but it's probably best not to go wandering – there's magic here to be sure, let's not put it to the test before we know what kind of magic, eh?'

He smiled at the look of shock still upon Maggie's face. She nodded in agreement.

The sudden squall of wind had died immediately when Maggie backed away from the stones – it was as if they didn't want her to come near them. Maggie shook her head; *stones don't have wants or needs, do they?* She had thought books didn't have feelings either, and that had been corrected today, so why not solid stone too? She suddenly had to hold in a giggle. This was mad!

'Right now, there's a group on the hill there–' Granda said and Maggie looked in the direction he pointed. 'There are ancient carvings over that way, I think. Well, they're ancient in our time – at the moment they're probably fresh!

Maggie smiled at Granda's excitement and the mixed-up, back-to-front timeline. 'I think we'll make our way over there and see what they're doing – see if we can find out a bit more about the place before we go looking or touching...' he raised an eyebrow at Maggie, but not in a too-serious or truly angry way.

'You're the boss, Granda!' Maggie grinned and they set off across the valley floor, carefully skirting the standing stones in the centre, in case they should "upset" them again.

Arriving at the foot of the hill they had seen from the glen, they began climbing up the heathery slope. It was hard work. As they drew level with the crowd Granda had seen, they could hear the low hum of voices. Granda pressed a finger to his lips, panting as quietly as he could. He took out his remote once more. The voices tuned in like a radio and suddenly made sense again, as they had done in the Mesolithic. This language was a bit different to that one, but still completely foreign to Maggie's ears, even though she could understand every word being said. She didn't think she'd ever get used to the sensation.

They made their way around a thick stand of bushes, hidden from the view of the people, but able to see them easily. It was the perfect vantage-point to observe what they were doing.

The crowd were gathered before a large, flat breadth of rock. They all faced it with reverence – Maggie could see it in their posture, how the main body of the crowd were silently watching. The voices they could hear came from a handful of people at the front, all of whom seemed to be involved in drawing upon the surface of the rock. "Drawing" wasn't quite the right description, Maggie thought - they were *carving* upon the stone. It must have taken a long time too, because there were deep, smooth cups with equally-deep rings surrounding some of them. It was as if the rock had been scooped out, like ice-cream from a tub. The effect of the rings made some of the cups look rather like targets, like something an archer might aim at. The people were focussed on one particular area, the cup here shallower than the others. This seemed to be a new addition to the art-work covering the rest of the rock.

'Wonder what it means, eh lassie?' Granda whispered very quietly in Maggie's ear. Maggie gazed at the markings, turning her head slowly, this way and that, screwing her eyes up then opening them wide, trying to let a pattern emerge from what at first-glance looked completely random. A bird caught her eye, soaring over the glen below, wings stretched wide as it floated on an updraft. Maggie suddenly made the connection between the rock-face, the valley stretched below and the positions of the standing-stones they had first seen.

'It's a map!' Maggie exclaimed, rather excitedly and rather loudly.

The people gathered round the rocks became abruptly aware that they were not alone. Almost as one, their heads lifted and snapped in the direction of Maggie and Granda, still peering through their thicket. Maggie gulped while Granda hastily pointed the remote at his own throat. The largest of the men in the group rounded on them, covering the distance in a few powerful strides.

'Peace to you,' Granda said in the same language the people were using, holding his hands up in the universal sign for "we are unarmed and we come in peace".

'Who are you and what is your business here? We do not recognise your faces or your dress,' the man asked in a deep, commanding voice. His hair was wiry and wavy, thick upon his head, a dark, red-tinged brown. It fell to his chin where it blended with a <u>russet</u> beard, covering the lower half of his face and throat. His eyebrows were heavy and low, frowning deep over narrowed eyes. He was not at all pleased at the <u>intrusion</u> of the strangers.

'We are visitors from a distant land,' Granda began, fumbling with the remote behind his right leg. A basket laden with fresh food appeared. Maggie could see what looked like corn on the cob, and a pile of bright orange lentils among its contents. She wondered if the Neoliths would accept a gift-basket. The <u>defensive</u> stances and menacing-looking axes they were gripping made her think not. Then she noticed Granda slipping the remote back into his pocket smoothly. He obviously didn't want it to be seen.

'We bring an offering of crops for your table,'
Granda continued, still speaking the same foreign
language.

'We have crops of our own,' the man said
dismissively. 'You are here without invitation,
how can we possibly trust you?'

A woman broke away from the group. She was
slightly shorter than the man (who seemed to be
in charge), but had an air of self-assurance and
power radiating from her. Her hair was also dark,
a warm shade of brown that made Maggie think of
Granda's favourite plain chocolate.

'Rungor, they mean no harm – he is old and has
brought a child,' she spoke in a deep voice too,
placing a hand on the arm of the chief that was
resting on his axe. He relaxed only slightly at her
touch, but it was obvious that they were equals in

terms of authority. 'I am Anacrua, this is my
companion, Rungor – we are the elders of this
land and people.'

Her eyes were an astonishing shade of pale blue,
and seemed to sparkle more than any other eyes
Maggie had ever seen. It was as if they were giving
off a glow, actively projecting light, like the beam
of a lighthouse. The woman met Maggie's awed
gaze and she had the sensation that the woman
was reading her thoughts. She smiled warmly.

'They mean no harm,' she repeated quietly,
directly addressing Rungor. He met and held her
gaze for a few long moments. Maggie held her
breath. She and Granda's lives could hang on his
decision to believe this Anacrua woman or not! At
long last, he nodded once, having seen something
in her eyes that must have convinced him. His
body language changed immediately.

'Arun, come receive the strangers' gift,' he called to a small boy Maggie hadn't noticed before. 'Our young one' he bowed his head as the boy stepped forward cautiously; he didn't seem to be quite as sure of their visitors. Maggie was still uneasy too – was it really going to be that easy? At this strange woman's word, they had been accepted unquestioned into the group. Was it a trick?

Thinking it would be helpful if she was polite, she lifted the basket and made her way towards the boy. In spite of her <u>consternation</u> over their current situation, Maggie couldn't help noticing that the boy had Anacrua's piercing eyes. He smiled shyly when Maggie placed the heavy basket in his outstretched arms. Her face felt suddenly hot. Granda raised his eyebrows, smiling <u>impishly</u> as Maggie returned to his side. Maggie's embarrassment only increased. Anacrua smiled too, cuffing Arun's head <u>affectionately</u> as he returned to her side.

'What have you brought?' Rungor spoke to Granda now.

'Oh there's some maize, or corn, that's the yellow and green, some lentils, that's the wee orange pile, and some flax which is good for making ropes and the like.'

'We know of this stuff you call flax, we call it by another name, but the others are new, thank-you. Our Seeing-Elder will inspect them, you say they grow in the ground, like barley?' Rungor asked.

Granda nodded and at Rungor's direction the basket was lifted by a young man who then disappeared into the crowd. Maggie wondered who (and what) the Seeing-Elder was, knowing it must mean someone, in some way, magical.

'Come, you must be hungry from your journey, we will return to the village and you can tell us more of your home-land,' Rungor said and motioned that Granda and Maggie should follow.

Anacrua took her place by his side, Arun between them and they led the way down the hillside, back in the direction of the standing-stones where Maggie and Granda had arrived. Maggie's tummy was still a bit knotted with uncertainty. Could this really be a trap? Were they really just going to feed them and have a chat? Maggie looked sideways at Granda, trying to gauge his thoughts on the unfolding events. He looked like he was having a ball, enjoying his day. If he wasn't worried then Maggie probably didn't have cause for concern, but she remained on alert. The only option she seemed to have was to allow themselves to be led from the hill and see what happened next, trusting in the remote's ability to help them out – she just wondered what else it might be capable of...

They returned to the Nether Largie stones, skirting the edge of the shape they made. Maggie was interested to see what the wind did now that they were escorted by the Neolithic inhabitants of the glen. The crowd bowed their heads <u>respectfully</u> as they passed – just like the stones with the carvings on the hill, these standing stones were sacred too, Maggie understood. From this angle, she could see that the pockmarks were similar cups-and-rings as the ones higher on the hill. They were obviously significant in the peoples' belief system. Maggie's curiosity was burning to know what they meant – more map-points? She also noticed that the wind remained calm as they passed, obviously their Neolithic guides were key. Maggie and Granda were strangers here – it seemed that the whole glen knew this, stones and all.

She and Granda followed Rungor and Anacrua towards a series of low buildings, nestled in the side of a rise to the North of the glen. It was a fair walk, but as they drew closer, Maggie could see that the buildings made up a small village. They were fairly long and low, with sloping roofs and walls made of timber. Smoke was rising from the centre of their roofs. There weren't many houses and as they entered the village properly, Maggie could see that the crowd from the rocks must have made up almost the entire community.

There were around forty people, at her best guess. Slightly more than the Mesolithic group, but still not large by modern standards. They all looked curiously at the visitors as they <u>dispersed</u> back into the village, some returning to their own houses, others going to tend fires or animals.

Maggie and Granda were led to the largest building in the village. It was made from wood like the others, but Maggie noticed that the walls were actually rows of straight, upright timbers, lined up side-by-side. The roof was a rounded, rectangular dome, and the building was long and low, similar to the village houses but on a much grander scale. It was so grand, in fact, that it couldn't really be called a house at all. It was closer, by far, to a small *hall*, maybe the size, Maggie thought, of the Scout Hall in a clearing in the woods in Gourock.

They entered at one end. It was dark, cool and quiet inside, the only light coming from the centre of the building. Maggie couldn't see the centre clearly; the light wasn't reaching them without <u>obstruction</u>. This was because the inside of the structure seemed to be split into separate areas, by <u>internal</u> timber walls.

Granda held Maggie's hand and the two of them were carefully quiet and respectful, for this was obviously an important place to the people of the village. The hush inside, and the way Rungor and Anacrua moved slowly and deliberately made Maggie think of a church. She supposed this must be exactly what this hall was to them.

Passing the first internal division, Maggie could see a raised platform piled high with grain. Some clay pots and containers were arranged neatly underneath. Moving into the central and biggest "room" in the building, Rungor and Anacrua invited Maggie and Granda to sit on the earthen floor. Granda had difficulty crossing his old legs, but eventually settled as Rungor began to speak:

'Before I tell you of our <u>customs</u>, please tell me of your homeland, have you travelled far?'

'Well...yes, you could say that,' Granda began. Maggie wondered how we would explain where they had come from. After a pause, with a look of decision on his face, he continued. 'We come from the future, see, not a distant land geographically, but distant in, well, in time.'

He was going for the truth then? Maggie wondered if this was entirely wise – how on earth would Rungor and Anacrua react to this admission?

'Anacrua knew this already, but thank you for your honesty,' Rungor said, bowing his shaggy head toward Granda, who nodded briefly back. Maggie felt her jaw hanging open slightly in surprise. Well then, it was as easy as that, was it? She fought the urge to laugh – Granda did always tell her that "honesty was the best policy".

Apart from her surprise at how well Rungor had taken this news, Maggie suspected that Anacrua must indeed be the Seeing-Elder, her own suspicions had been correct too! There was magic afoot alright. Damping down the excitement this idea caused, Maggie tried to take in everything else as she listened to the adults. She noticed, for example, that the light-source was a perfect circle in the ceiling, through which she could see the clear blue sky outside. Projecting from it was a beam of light, cutting through the very centre of the room, while the outskirts and corners were left in deep shadow.

There was a large, flat stone on the floor within the circle of light, more of a slab than anything else. Carved upon it was the same cup-and-ring mark they had seen on the rocks and standing stones in the glen. Maggie knew instinctively that when the sun reached the middle of the sky at noon, the cup would be directly filled with a beam of light. It seemed to be a running theme, circles and beams of sunlight and the middle of the day and year. It made sense, really, that people who relied on the sun would be focussed so meticulously on it.

She realised that her fear had disappeared – these people weren't violent or trying to trick them, they really were just welcoming of complete strangers – and time-travelling strangers, no less – into their villages, their sacred places. Maggie thought that maybe the people in her own time could learn a thing or two from these Neoliths.

'And who is your companion?' Rungor's attention now turned to Maggie, who was snapped out of her observations at once and began to feel a little squirmy under his gaze. She looked to Granda to keep talking.

'This is my Granddaughter, Maggie,' Granda said, smiling down at her encouragingly.

'"Grand"- daughter? What is the connection then? She is your own child?'

'Ah no, her mother is my child, Maggie's sort of my child, once-removed–'

'Removed? You removed her from her mother?' Rungor looked puzzled; the family-member titles in the Neolithic were obviously exceedingly different from the present-day.

'No, no! Maggie's mother is my child, Maggie is what we call my Grandchild, I didn't remove her from anyone!' Granda was chuckling a little.

'Ah, I understand, we of course have different names for family members here,' Rungor nodded sagely. 'You speak our tongue well, though.'

Granda met Maggie's eyes briefly, still smiling. 'What is your time like?' Rungor asked.

'Well it's a lot different to yours – it's much busier, there are a lot more people and buildings and things. We have a lot of new technology – too much, really, can't keep up with it anymore myself.'

'Technology?' the word was evidently alien to Rungor.

'Well now, how to put this the right way...'
Granda huffed at little; there was a fine line
between explaining the advances of the future
and <u>potentially</u> insulting the way of life in the
Neolithic. 'There are lots of new tools, some with
moving parts of their own, powered by fuels...'
Granda motioned to the fine stone axe hanging
from Rungor's belt but trailed off slightly. 'And,
with these new tools – machines, they're called –
there are lots of different ways of doing things,
everything moves quicker, people are carried
about in vehicles with wheels and engines and...'

It was <u>vague</u> but seemed to be enough
explanation for Rungor, who raised his hand and
nodded again.

'Mysteries, I'm sure to us, but the concern of
others to come,' Rungor seemed to be happy in

his own time. 'Our ways are just as mysterious to you, yes?'

He was a wise man; Maggie could see that. Granda agreed and Rungor continued:

'Now I will tell you a little of our ways. We are land-tenders and animals-keepers – we grow crops and animals and gather foods from the earth. As you have seen, there are many of us...'

Maggie realised that a community of this size must still have been large in Prehistoric times. She thought of cities like Glasgow, and how many people lived there, wondering what the Neolithic people would make of Buchanan Street on a Saturday afternoon.

'...This glen is an ancient and sacred land, a place of great power and mystery. You have joined us on the most <u>hallowed</u> day of the year – the summer solstice, the longest day. Anacrua assures me that this has been written in the stars – you were <u>destined</u> to join us this day,' Rungor went on.

Maggie and Granda's eyes met and Granda gave her a wink – he had been right, as usual! Maggie then looked to Anacrua who was sitting with her eyes closed, her wrists resting on her crossed knees, apparently sleeping, or <u>communing</u> with some higher power. Maggie's eyes had by now adjusted to the lower light inside the large timber building. She could see that in each of Anacrua's hands she held some kind of stone ball.

They were certainly round-ish, but one had many nodules on its surface, so that it might move a bit like dice, (although with many more faces), if it was cast down. The other had several faces too, though these were larger than the first, looking almost like the smooth, flat tops of a mushroom. Anacrua was spinning them slowly in her slim, long-fingered hands, each just about the size of her palm. Maggie was deeply intrigued but didn't think she was brave enough to ask what they were – or what they were for. Maybe she'd find out as their visit progressed.

For the first time, Maggie also noticed that their gift-basket was sitting in the shadow at the edge of the room. So Anacrua *was* the Seeing-Elder – she had to be! Maggie was even more in awe of her than before.

Coming out of whatever trance-like state she'd been in, Anacrua smiled at Maggie and Granda in turn before saying: 'Today we celebrate our god, the Sun, who gives life to everything and everyone here. At sunset we feast, then there will be much dancing, until the sun rises once more and we bless the year to come.'

Maggie realised that this was a bit like Hogmanay then – a celebration of the New Year, even though it was high-summer here, rather than midwinter when Maggie would be celebrating New Year's Eve at home.

They emerged from the building soon after. Maggie had had to pull Granda to his feet since his legs had stiffened up from sitting cross-legged. He was now hobbling due to the pins-and-needles in his toes. The rest of the village was busily preparing for the feast Anacrua had spoken of and the sun was already beginning to sink lower in the sky, staining it a blazing, brilliant orange.

'It is time!' Rungor called, voice carrying over the whole village.

CHAPTER NINE

As a <u>procession</u>, they all made their way to the centre of the village, where a large fire was being <u>stoked</u> into life. Rungor seated Granda and Maggie beside himself and Anacrua, a place of great honour, Maggie felt. Granda seemed to think so too and he was looking both pleased with the arrangement, and a little embarrassed. They didn't have time to discuss this, however, because next second, with a great, <u>keening</u> shout, six <u>burly</u> men appeared from the big hall. They carried between them what looked like a large, wooden raft, laden with bowls of steaming-hot food.

Smaller pottery bowls were passed around and the food shared out to everyone. Maggie looked nervously at Granda who was already tucking into his bowlful, talking easily with Rungor as if they were old friends. Maggie nibbled on some of the meat. It tasted like steak and was deliciously smoky in flavour. In fact, all of the food was tasty, she found, and was soon full and sleepy, leaning a little against Granda's arm.

'Good grub eh?' Granda smacked his lips after a third helping of steak. Maggie grinned up at him. There was more than enough food for everyone; they were obviously skilled farmers, even at this stage in Prehistory. Granda finished eating at last and looked thoughtfully towards the stone cross in the distance.

'There's a standing stone in Gourock, y'know, lassie?' he said.

'Really?!' Maggie was amazed – she'd never seen it before. 'Where is it? Can we go see it when we get home?'

'We can indeed, it's near my bowling club, sitting on the cliff above Kempock Street. People call it 'Granny Kempock's Stane,' Granda explained. 'Sailors on the Clyde used to come and make offerings at it, in the old days, like, to give them good weather and fortune on the sea. Young couples used to bless their marriages by dancing round it.'

Maggie was enthralled – all that history right on her doorstep! 'When does it date from?' she asked, wondering if it could be as old as Kilmartin's stones.

'Oh well now, no one's all that sure, but sometimes it's given a Bronze Age date of about 2000 BC – we'll be visiting the Bronze Age another day, no doubt. But then, some people think Granny Kempock dates to around the same time as Gourock Castle–'

'Gourock has a castle?!' Maggie nearly choked on her food. She'd never known that! How could she have lived her whole life in Gourock and not known that there was a castle to explore?

'Well it *did* have a castle – nothing remains of it now, lass, not even a ruin, just a wee mound in Darroch Park,' Granda said, smiling at Maggie's outburst.

That explained it. Yet Maggie was sad that she couldn't go and see even the ruins of it. Maybe in another book they'd get a chance to visit the castle when it was still standing! She asked Granda this and he said he didn't see why not. Maggie was looking forward to it already!

'There's some cup-and-ring markings in Gourock too, y'know?' Granda added causally.

'Where?!' So much history in her own hometown, why hadn't she taken interest before now?

'On the golf course,' Granda said. 'There's a fair few cup-marked rocks out Loch Thom way too...'

Maggie and Granda often visited Gourock Golf Club, (and Loch Thom, for that matter). Granda had a social membership because his house was only a short walk away from the clubhouse. He and Maggie dropped in now and again for a cold drink and a chocolate bar. They'd had Maggie's Mum's birthday party there too. Maggie liked the club; it was warm and comfortable and had wonderful views over the river to Argyll. Granda would tell her the lovely Gaelic names of the hills while they sat in the comfy leather chairs at the big windows. The bar staff were always friendly too.

'We could go and see them, I know the Greenkeeper remember,' he gave Maggie a wink. 'We'd just have to make sure the course was quiet, maybe on a wet day or right early in the morning – it would be ok as long as we had permission.'

'Yes please!' Maggie said. 'Are they like the ones we've seen here? Was Gourock a sacred place too, Granda?'

'I'm not sure Maggie, it might have been – we can go and take a look and see what we think, eh?'

Now Maggie was not only looking forward to their next Magic Bookcase adventure – wherever that took them – but also to going home and exploring the historical sites in Gourock that she had, before now, never known about.

'There's bits of history all over Gourock – all over Inverclyde more widely, Maggie – all over *everywhere*, for that matter, as we'll learn. It just needs to be looked for...' Granda said, patting her back warmly. She grinned and continued eating, feeling that she was on the brink of a whole lifetime's worth of adventures.

The sun had set as they ate. Maggie watched the sky turning all the wonderful red, orange and pink shades of sunset before an inky, velvety night settled around the feasters. As she sat there, the stars began to come out until they were scattered thickly across the deep, violet sky.

Maggie had never seen so many stars! They covered the heavens like a blanket or a fine layer of powdery snow, their light twinkling merrily in time with the crackling flames of the fire. She had learned about light-pollution at school and realised that there were no electric lights anywhere in this world to pollute this sky. Even in the light from the fire, there were many more stars than Maggie had ever seen before. It was a sight to remember forever.

She felt comfortable and content sitting in front of the fire listening to Rungor and Anacrua's deep, soothing voices.

'Would you like to hear our story, Maggie? The story of how we came to be here?' Anacrua asked.

Maggie nodded, 'Yes, please.'

'We revere the Sun, young Maggie, because she gives us everything in life. Even the land we live on was given by the Sun,' Rungor began. 'Many moons ago, a great many seasons of Plenty and Hunger, the land was covered by The Great Ice. Nothing could live here except the White Bears and even the bears for only some of the moon-cycles. The Sun came and with great effort and time, she cleared all the ice, sent it in retreat and gave us Land to live on. It was the beginning of All Things...'

Maggie was drawn into the story instantly, but then Anacrua lifted a hand and drew some of the fire's smoke towards her. Maggie watched in amazement. It was like some kind of weird magnet, drawn <u>irresistibly</u> to Anacrua's dancing fingers.

'...First the Plants came,' Anacrua fashioned the smoke into a field of dancing grass, rolling like waves in an invisible wind; then a great forest grew at double-speed, trees forcing their way towards the sky. '...then the Wing-Fliers...', flocks of smoke-birds fluttered over the grass and through the trees. '...then the Foragers, then the Great Grazers,' small animals now scurried and scampered happily among the trees before being joined by majestic deer, grazing on the smoke-grass in a large herd.

'The Sun filled the land with food and made it good for people to come and live. Our ancestors arrived, seeking new land, living differently to us...' The smoke animals now formed smoothly into human figures very familiar to Maggie. '...It was a time when the earth and sea held more, because of the Sun's power. The Ancestors moved around, never settling for long in one place, but using the land with the phases of the Moon and Sun, always moving like the two great orbs. They were successful but it was a hard life.'

Maggie had seen that very life for herself – in the Mesolithic!

'Then one day,' Anacrua now took up the story, the smoke growing suddenly darker, swirling in a thick ball before her, waiting for its next form. 'A young and foolish hunter became greedy and killed an Akvil Stag. There was an agreement, you see, of all the people in the Land that the Akvil Stag would never be killed. They understood that the deer herds needed him to keep growing every year. He was the giver of life to the deer – he was the Gift Stag, given directly from the Sun herself...'

The smoke turned into a magnificent stag, antlers held proudly like a crown on his shaggy head. '…But the Young Hunter wanted the glory of taking down the great animal. He was focussed only on trying to prove to his tribe that he was the hunter his Elder had been…'

The figure of a young man now knelt beside the fallen form of the deer, leaning on his spear, looking down at his prize with a defeated slump to his shoulders – he regretted it, Maggie realised, but had a feeling that it was too late for that.

'Upon the killing of the stag, the Sun summoned the Water into The Great Wave…' the smoke spread and grew, turning into a massive tidal-wave. Maggie could almost hear the roar of the water. '…It crashed into the Land and swept away many camps, killing many people. The Sun was angry and punished the people for the greed of the Young Hunter. The waters took some of the Land back and soon the old, reliable hunting-grounds in the East became a sea, no longer full of land-animals and places to live.' The smoke now took on a familiar shape – roughly the outline that Maggie knew as the British Isles. 'The Land we live on now became an island, all on its own, isolated and cut-off from the vast hunting plains the people once knew, from friends they had loved.

And so The Land Beyond took its name – it was the land beyond the sea. The hunting grounds had shrunk greatly and the people went hungrier than they had for many moons. They had to find new ways of gathering food.

Scyth the Elder journeyed a far distance and brought back The Knowledge – the ways of farming the land. We learned a new way to use the Sun's gifts and in time she forgave the Young Hunter's <u>folly</u>, coming to shine strongly again. We have everything here because of her and we know not to take more than the Sun can replenish in her cycles. She doesn't become angry if we understand the fine balance we live in. It is the most important lesson we pass on to our Young Ones. They must learn from the mistakes of the past, learn the ways of the Land and the proper traditions to thank the Sun for her gifts. That is why we come together at the solstice – to give offerings and dance to the Sun within her stones'

Maggie watched Anacrua's smoke re-join the fire, thinking about the story she'd just heard. "The Great Ice", was the Ice Age, she understood, fascinated to hear it from the perspective of the Neolithic people. It was so interesting to hear the stories that helped them make sense of their world. It was different to what Maggie was taught as religion, but that didn't matter too much. She could appreciate the Neolithic ways, understand them even, despite them being so unlike her own.

The last of the bowls were now being collected from the feasters. Rungor rose and everyone followed. Granda caught Maggie's eye with an excited expression on his face.

'Something tells me, Maggie-Moo, that we're about to see something special!' he said, squeezing her shoulders as they were swept along in the crowd of their Neolithic companions.

Rungor offered his arm to Anacrua who took it gracefully, leading the people down into the glen. Instead of heading to the Nether Largie stone cross, they veered to the right, and Maggie saw in the light of another blazing fire, that they were heading this time for a *circle* of standing stones. The fire was dancing in the centre of the circle. The group filed inside and spread out, forming their own circle between the stones and the fire. Anacrua spoke:

'We come together this night to praise the Sun, our life-source, who always gives and takes nothing in return. The Sun, in her <u>wondrous</u> orb, reminds us that there is no beginning and no end to her cycle, every year she returns to grow our crops so that we may feed ourselves and our animals. We come together to give her praise...'

At her signal, two men and two women stepped forward, each carrying what looked like a large, clay pot. At points around the fire, four deep holes had been dug, a neat mound of earth piled up beside them. The men and women carried their pots carefully to one of the holes and knelt down. They placed them gently in the ground and stood straight once more.

As one, the assembled crowd took voice, saying 'With the Sun, from the Earth, it came, and to the Earth we now return it, bless the days to come.'

Maggie understood – this was the people thanking the sun for providing the earth with the animals and crops they'd raised. Each pot must contain some of the food and drink that they'd all feasted on, and now it was being returned as a gift and an offering back to the land. The land was being fed, just as they had been.

The men and women now heaped the earth back in on top of the pots, the crowd watchful and silent. This was an important part of the evening, Maggie understood. On top of two neat handprints left in the soil atop each buried pot, one of the mysterious stone balls that Maggie had seen earlier in the day were placed. She longed to know what they were for, but before she could try and have a proper look, Anacrua stood and motioned to another group of men and women who were approaching the stone circle. They were all carrying what looked like large drums, made from wood and animal skins. What made the line-up remarkable, however, were the headdresses they were wearing. Each drummer wore the horns of an animal: the man in front wore an enormous set of deer antlers. Another man wore long, pointed horns that made Maggie think of buffalos, and the woman wore a curly set of ram's horns. They looked quite battered and must have been part of a long tradition. The point of one of the ram's horns was blunt and a couple of the antler-tines were missing or splintered.

This must be in respect to the animals they've always hunted, Maggie thought. *They respect them for providing the people with food, like Anacrua said.*

The crowd parted as the musicians filed into the centre of the circle, taking up places around the large bonfire in the middle. And they began to play.

Maggie had never heard anything like it; the drums boomed so loudly that she could feel the rhythm in her chest. The tempo increased steadily, until the arms of the musicians were nothing more than glowing blurs in the firelight. The effect was hypnotic; Maggie was swaying unconsciously to the beat. Suddenly, with a great reverberating BOOM-BOOM, the drummers ceased. The following silence was absolute except for the crackling fire. Then Rungor and Anacrua bellowed 'We dance!' and the crowd moved as one as the drummers struck up once more.

Maggie and Granda were carried along in the throng. The dance was synchronised and larger-than-life, the villagers leaping and spinning like gazelles or ballerinas or swallows in the air, Maggie couldn't pick just one description. They were singing a joyful, driving melody, thick with harmony and drum-beats, the summer air filled with the sound and the feverish, restlessness of the fire. The atmosphere was <u>intoxicating</u>, Granda's face was alight and shining with exertion and wonder.

The dancing continued all night, Maggie wasn't sure where her tiredness from earlier had gone, but she seemed to have more energy the longer they danced. Everyone was laughing merrily, dancing with <u>enthusiasm</u>, enjoying their celebrations without <u>restraint</u>. Then with another great BOOM-BOOM that Maggie could hear echoing around the whole glen, everyone stopped dancing as one, turning to face the East: the sun was beginning to rise.

It happened gradually, the deep, dark night lightening by degrees, the sky turning a paler lilac-streaked pink, before the first beams of sunlight crested the horizon. Maggie looked out over the glen, towards the stone cross. As the sunlight moved across the land, it hit each standing-stone. Like a stone skiffing across a loch, the light bounced from one to the next in great, glowing arcs. It soared through the air from the cross towards the circle in which they all stood, hitting the first stone and springing to the next. The tops all seemed to glow as if they were on fire, the light beginning to <u>refract</u> into a great, domed web over the crowd in the middle. The small stone balls atop each of the buried pots had beams of light snaking brightly from them too, twisting into the air to tangle with its fellows. Maggie knew she was witnessing some ancient magic at work. Today she'd learned that some things didn't necessarily have a sensible, 'normal' explanation. Some things were just, well, magical.

The effect of the sun on the stone was <u>entrancing</u> as it continued to rise over the land.

And that was the whole point of the celebration, Maggie understood – that the sun rose every single morning to give the people light and warmth and the ability to feed their families. It was indeed a glorious sight to see, the sun rising steadily over the joyful, but now-silent crowd, enclosed in a lattice of its light.

The sunrise progressed, the dome of light growing stronger. Then Rungor and Anacrua raised their hands above their heads, index fingers and thumbs making a circle. Everyone else followed suit and as one they lowered themselves to the ground, kneeling in worship before the sun. Maggie and Granda joined in – it would have been disrespectful not to. As the people got back to their feet, the sun now blazing, fully-risen from the horizon, they began to hug one another, wishing each other a prosperous New Year. Even Maggie and Granda were embraced by what felt like every single villager. The sunlight-dome faded as it continued to climb, the solstice over for another year. The crowd slowly made its way back towards the village. Rungor and Anacrua embraced Maggie and Granda once more and Maggie knew this was where their Neolithic adventure would end.

'Peace and light be with you always,' Anacrua placed a palm against their foreheads.

'Eh right, thanks, same to you,' Granda gruffed in reply, his cheeks pink. Maggie grinned. Then Arun ran to Maggie and hugged her tightly. Now it was Maggie's cheeks that were glowing and Granda who was grinning. Maggie nudged him embarrassedly.

'Before you go, Maggie, I'd like to give you a gift – something I think might come in…useful, in your future,' Anacrua smiled at the shocked but delighted expression spreading across Maggie's face.

Seemingly from thin-air, Anacrua produced one of the carved stone balls. Maggie felt a huge thrill of excitement – she would finally know what they were for. She didn't think she should say 'what is it?' so settled for a heartfelt 'Thank you' instead, as Anacrua placed the small but heavy artefact in Maggie's palm. It was curiously warm, like it had been sitting in front of the fire for a while, and Maggie could feel a strange kind of vibration from it, just the tiniest sense of <u>unceasing</u> movement. It was as if the stone were restless and wished to be on the move, or it had some softly-stirring creature inside it like an egg.

'You are wondering what it is for,' Anacrua said kindly. Maggie gave a sheepish nod, still thrilled with the gift she'd been given, whether it actually *did* anything or not. 'Our stones – the callachan – have a great many uses; they hold ancient magic. This one will help to *concentrate* power...'

Maggie was not, in truth, any less confused by this cryptic explanation, but nodded all the same. She had the feeling, (though she wasn't sure where it was coming from), that she would learn what the ball was for at some undefined future-point, that it wasn't too important to understand all at once.

She grinned widely at Anacrua, who nodded and said 'Use it well, I have no doubt you will.'

Then with a small bow from each of them, Rungor and Anacrua linked arms once more, ready to return to their lives, Arun skipping ahead. They all smiled at each other, strangers from vastly different lives, but somehow with understanding linking them all together. Turning their backs, the chiefs of the village walked slowly home and Maggie and Granda turned back towards the place they had first arrived, just beyond the boundary of the stone cross.

'Think on it like this, Maggie,' Granda began, sitting on a large boulder and beckoning her closer. 'There are no written records here, like we said earlier, no books – the cup-and-ring carvings are some of the only ways of recording things. We don't know exactly how people lived and carried out their daily lives. But the earth, the land they lived on, contains clues and secrets, waiting to be discovered that give us vague idea. In a way, everything *is* written, not with a pen and paper, but on the landscape itself.'

Maggie liked this – it was very poetic, in a way,

'Do you remember how we talked about the glaciers and the Ice Age?'

Maggie nodded, rolling her gift from Anacrua between her hands, unable to stop playing with it.

'Well, the shape of the land as it stands now tells us where the glaciers were, how they moved. The hills and glens of Scotland tell a story; they tell us how they came to be, just by looking the way they look and standing where they stand. In the same way, almost, everything that Prehistoric people left behind, especially the big stuff like these standing stones in Kilmartin, ruins of houses and all the other stuff Archaeologists have uncovered – everything is sitting there, like the writing in a book, giving us clues as to what Prehistory was actually like. Amazing, really, when you think about it, am I right?'

Maggie agreed whole-heartedly, it had been an amazing adventure. She had learned so much that she would have had a harder time understanding before today, because she had been able to see examples of it all first-hand (*sort-of*, she thought). Now she grasped the idea of Prehistory having no books or writing. She understood the gaps in what was actually *knowable* and she had enjoyed seeing the interpretation of the author of this particular book in which she found herself. The thought was still thrilling; they were *in* a book! She was suddenly exhausted.

'Enough for one day?' Granda smiled down at Maggie, who nodded, stifling a yawn. 'Right then, let's get back – your Mum and Dad will be coming for tea soon anyway...'

Maggie had forgotten all about the real time; she wondered how long ago they had left Granda's living-room. What a birthday this had been! She was, however, slightly puzzled as to how they would now leave the book – jumping in was all very well – it was downhill – but how on earth were they going to jump back out?

'Right then, stand by me here,' Granda lined Maggie up at his right side, taking her hand once more. 'On the count of three, jump as hard as you can and kick off into the air, got it?' Maggie nodded, <u>readying</u> herself, thinking of the villagers' dancing.

'One!' Maggie bent her knees, the small, warm lump of her magic stone callachan safe in her jeans-pocket.

'Two!' Granda gave her hand a reassuring squeeze.

'Three!' Maggie slammed her feet into the ground and straightened her legs, forcing herself into the air with all her might, wondering if she was powerful enough to manage...

And they were leaving Kilmartin behind, soaring into the air, the whole glen opening under them as they shot upwards. With the same twisting sensation as the descent into the book, (though now spinning in the opposite direction), the scene dissolved into a great, thunderous swirl of words, both written and heard.

Just as suddenly as before, Maggie and Granda found themselves thrown back into the living-room, swaying slightly to keep their balance. The book's pages fluttered before it slammed closed. Granda lifted it carefully from the rug and walked back to the bookcase. Maggie followed, quiet and solemn in respect to both the book and the magic of the bookcase to which she was now <u>privy</u>. Granda replaced the volume in its space and it glowed slightly with a dusty light for a few seconds as the bookcase welcomed it home.

'Quite something, eh?' Granda smiled, gently running his hands over the spines of the books and the solid wood of the magical piece of furniture. 'Anything else you'd like to know, Maggie?'

There was so much she wanted to know, but Maggie just grinned and said, 'Where to next?'

GLOSSARY

CHAPTER ONE

anticipation – eagerness, expectation, excitement

mischievous – playful, up to no-good

ornate – highly decorated

intricately – with lots of detail, very complex

tome – a large and heavy book

garishly – overly bright

solemn – serious, formal, with dignity

senile – weak and forgetful through old age

sceptical – disbelieving, unconvinced, doubtful

integrity – honesty, honour, having a strong sense of right and wrong

tenement-close – (a Scottish word) a building that housed many families in one- or two-room apartments. The hallways and staircases in these buildings were known as 'closes', often many families shared one toilet in this 'close' (the 's' is soft, like the 's' in *snake*, not a 'z' as in *zebra*, or when you 'close the door').

Chapter Two

squinted – looked with partly-closed eyes, as you would if looking at a bright light, for instance

locate – find

precise – exact or specific

transferred – moved from one place to another

half-heartedness – doing something without energy or interest

deliberately – done on purpose; consciously, intentionally

chute – a slide

garble – a confused, jumbled sound

melding – mixing and blending together

tangible – solid, touchable

Chapter Three

dappling – marked with different patches of colour or light. For example, a horse can be 'dappled grey-white'; it will be mottled, spotted or speckled with a mix of grey and white

cryptic – unclear, mysterious, puzzling

pioneers – the first people in a place; explorers, discoverers understatement – when something is a lot more, in this case difficult, than the words used to describe them. Describing someone who is six-foot-four-inches tall as 'quite tall' is an understatement, for example.

Mesolithic – the Middle Stone Age, which occurred between around 10,000 BC - 5,000 BC in Scotland

Palaeolithic – the Old Stone Age, which happened in Scotland before 10,000 BC; the last Ice Age

uninhabited – with no people in it, unpopulated

comprehension – understanding

undoubtedly – without a doubt, without question, certainly, definitely

CHAPTER FOUR

emanating – coming out of, starting from

unnerving – unsettling, strange, a little scary

telepathic – able to read minds, psychic

ancestor – something that came before (usually someone – ancestors are past family members) materialised – appeared from nowhere, came into being

contraption – device, gadget

scrutinising – looking closely, examining

disembodied – without a body, ghostly

vigorously – with energy or force

sensation – feeling

guffawed – laughed roughly

hampering – making more difficult, hindering

crustaceans – a type of small animal that has a hard shell covering its body, made up of segments with many legs. Many crustaceans live in water, for example: crabs, limpets, shrimp, lobster, barnacles. Others, like woodlice, live on dry land.

industrious – hard-working, productive

CHAPTER FIVE

tine – point, spike. Forks have individual spikes – these are called tines, as well as the individual points of a deer's antlers

precaution – a safety measure, a safeguard, protection

reconstructed – recreated, rebuilt from leftover pieces and ideas

Archaeologists – Academics whose main concern is the recovery, protection and interpretation of prehistoric artefacts and remains. They often dig these remains from the ground very carefully

interpretations – explanations based on evidence – in archaeology this evidence can include things that have been found in the ground or elsewhere. Ideas about how things worked based on these findings

suppress – hold back, hold in, damp down

CHAPTER SIX

suspended – hanging, hovering

ceasing – ending, finishing

momentum – movement, motion, energy

hindrance – delay, difficulty

Neolithic – the New Stone Age, which occurred in Scotland between 4,000 and 2,000 BC

transition – changeover, a shift, move towards something new

substantial – sturdy, large

Passover – Jewish festival celebrated in the Spring, celebrating the freeing of the Hebrew slaves from Egypt

Diwali – Hindu festival of lights, celebrated in the Autumn each year on the darkest night (the night of the new moon). People light many lanterns and other lights, wear their best clothes and have a big celebration

ceremonies – services – formal procedures people take part in for special occasions, for example a Wedding ceremony

rituals – similar to ceremonies – formal practices people carry out but perhaps on a more day-to-day basis

serenely – calmly, happily, peacefully

pock-marked – dimpled, with holes or marks on it

CHAPTER SEVEN

vantage-point – look-out post with some advantage or other – in this case that it was hidden but provided a view. Other advantages might be that the position is high enough to see over a large area below

reverence – admiration, respect, in worship

updraft – a current of air rising upwards from the
ground

russet – red-brown in colour

intrusion – interruption, interference

defensive – wary, cautious, protective

projecting – coming from, being sent outwards

awed – amazed, impressed, respectful

consternation – anxiety, worry, concern

impishly – mischievously, playfully

affectionately – with care and love, tenderly,
warmly

CHAPTER EIGHT

respectfully – politely, courteously; considerate of
other people's feelings, beliefs or opinions

dispersed – spread out

obstruction – a barrier, an obstacle

internal – inside, the opposite of external or
outside

customs – traditions, habits or practices people
follow

instinctively – knowing something without needing obvious proof, something you feel like you 'just know' automatically. You can talk about a parent's instinct, where parents 'just know' how to look after their babies, or a hunting instinct, where wild animals 'just know' how to hunt to feed themselves

meticulously – specifically, carefully, accurately, particularly

sagely – wisely

technology – a word that holds a few different, but linked meanings – it can refer to individual pieces of technology, such as computers, laptops, mobile phones and so on, but equally refers to the "simpler" tools of the prehistoric communities – their axes etc. were as much technology to them as a computer is to us. Technology can also refer to the knowledge and expertise by which tools, computers etc. are made and used

potentially – possibly, something that might happen

vague – unclear or indefinite

hallowed – holy, important, sacred

destined – meant to be or intended to happen

communing – connecting with, communicating, talking to

CHAPTER NINE

procession – a formal walk, march or parade

stoked – stirred up and made stronger, for a fire this might involve putting on more wood or fuel, or blowing on it to give it more oxygen to burn brighter and longer

keening – loud, sharp, echoing

burly – well-built, strong and broad, muscular

irresistibly – uncontrollably

orbs – an orb is a sphere – a ball

folly – foolishness, recklessness

CHAPTER TEN

wondrous – amazing, impressive, astounding

tempo – rhythm, beat, speed

hypnotic – spellbinding, mesmerising, fascinating

reverberating – echoing, rumbling

throng – crowd, mob or mass, in this case, of people

synchronised – at the same time, all at once, coordinated

intoxicating – strong and impossible to resist

exertion – effort and energy

enthusiasm – with eagerness and interest, passionately

restraint – holding back, limited – 'without restraint' is without holding back, with no limit

refract – bend

entrancing – like hypnotic – engrossing, spellbinding

prosperous – bountiful, full of success and good luck, in this case, full of good food and crops

embraced – hugged, held, cuddled

unceasing – without end, constant

beckoning – motioning or signalling someone to come closer, summoning

whole-heartedly – completely, passionately

readying – preparing

privy – in the know, in on the secret

MAGGIE'S MAP OF SCOTLAND

1. THE MESOLITHIC PEOPLE IN THE
STORY WERE CAMPING SOMEWHERE AROUND HERE

2. THE ISLAND OF RUM, WHERE THE
MESOLITHIC PEOPLE WENT TO COLLECT
BLOODSTONE

3. KILMARTIN GLEN, HOME OF THE NEOLITHIC
PEOPLE MAGGIE AND GRANDA MEET

4. MAES HOWE TOMB ON ORKNEY

Maggie's Artefact Appendix

Mesolithic Mattock
- a digging tool

Mesolithic Harpoon

Nether Largie's Middle Standing Stone
as it stands today
-speckled with lichen,
weathered and faded,
its cup-and-ring markings are
nonetheless still visible and extensive

Maggie's Callachan
- a neolithic carved stone ball

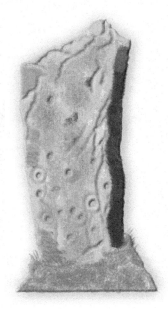

Rungor's Neolithic Axe

Finding Out More...

Here you'll find some suggestions for finding out further information on the topics covered in this book. Just remember to be safe on the internet! Make sure you have your parent or guardian's permission before you log on and never give out personal information, like your name, age, address or school to anyone online. If you aren't happy with a website, if something feels 'off' to you, tell someone you trust right away. It's always better to be safe than sorry!

That being said, there is a wealth of further information on the web and it can be a great resource. If you've enjoyed this book and want to find some more information on the Stone Ages in Scotland, why not look-up some of the terms from the *Prehistoric Prologue,* like Palaeolithic, Mesolithic or Neolithic.

THINGS TO THINK ABOUT:

Granda mentions that 'a great forest' once covered Scotland and this is perfectly true. 'The Caledonian Forest' blanketed the country after the last Ice Age. Due to a number of factors – climate change and human activity among the most important – the forest receded greatly. However, there are still patches of it to be found in modern Scotland, that is, descendants of the original trees still growing in some areas. Why not find out where these are and visit the important trees – part of the natural heritage of Scotland, representing 9000 years of growth!

Granda talks about the Mesolithic people using *curraghs* and *coracles*, why not search for these boats and see for yourself what they looked like. Curraghs are still made and used in some parts of Ireland. In a later book coracles will appear again, in connection with the famous Scottish Saint,

Columba of Iona. Why not try making a model with some fallen twigs and sticks. It would be better to use a pair of old tights or leggings, or even a t-shirt, instead of an animal skin, however! And remember to ask permission before you cut up your own or someone else's clothes!

What do you think the cup-and-ring markings meant? Remember no one knows for sure, so there are no real 'right or wrong' answers. Could they have been maps? Or ways of writing down place-names or distances? Try to get into the mind-set of someone from Prehistory – with no books, internet or electricity, what would be important to you? What would concern you most about the world you lived in? How would you try to make sense of things that seemed to have an invisible cause like the weather, the seasons, even the time of day?

Maggie thinks of 'buffalo' when she sees one of the Neolithic head-dresses on the head of a drummer at the feast. See if you can find out the name of the prehistoric animal these sorts of horns are likely to have come from – they are the ancestors of modern cows.

Maggie is amazed to learn that Gourock has a standing stone and rock-carvings of its own (this is true in real-life!). Why not try to find out if there have been any Prehistoric artefacts or structures found near where you live?

Look up the Orkney Neolithic village of Skara Brae and Isbister, the 'Tomb of the Eagles' – these are amazing sites of great archaeological importance and give a unique insight into the lives of our Neolithic ancestors. They show that Neolithic people built furniture – beds, seats, even display cabinets for cooking and eating utensils – and lived a life not too dissimilar to our modern ones, even such a long time ago!

Maggie receives a 'callachan' from Anacrua, a magical stone ball with, (as of yet), unknown powers. These are real artefacts from the Scottish Neolithic (although, I've made up the name 'callachan'). No one knows what they were for – they could have been a form of currency, (that is, money), used for swapping and buying. Maybe they were symbols of status – objects that belonged to the chiefs of villages and groups of people. What do you think? There are some examples on the National Museum of Scotland's website, why not go and have a look for yourself?

There is a lot of Neolithic material that couldn't be included in *The Prehistoric Prologue* – there's just not enough time or space to explain everything about the era. Why not look-up *Cursus* and *Henge* Monuments and see what you can find out – these are later Neolithic monuments of great significance for Scottish prehistory.

WHY NOT VISIT:

Kilmartin Glen – located in Argyll, between Oban and Lochgilphead. It's about two hours by car from Glasgow on the A816 and is very visitor-friendly. You'll probably need sturdy boots or wellies as the glen is mostly covered in grass. Access is free and there is free parking nearby. There's also a museum, open between March and December (it closes over Christmas until March 1st), which has a small entrance fee. Kilmartin Glen features many ancient sites of interest, with over 5000 years of history represented – Maggie and Granda even return to the area in Book Three to see the coronation of a Gaelic King!

Or if you're feeling really adventurous, you could travel to Orkney Neolithic Village!

If you are visiting any site or come across something you think might be an ancient artefact remember to treat it with respect. It is a good idea to leave things where you found them, disturbing them as little as possible. Always follow the Scottish Outdoor Access Code (SOAC) – for example, don't leave litter behind or take anything away from sites. For more information on this you can look-up the SOAC on the internet. Our country is beautiful but we have to look after it to keep it that way.

With special thanks to Gerry McDade,
whose enthusiasm and guidance encouraged me to
take the plunge and get this book into print.

Everyone needs a mentor, I'm glad to call Gerry mine.

Look out for more adventures with
Maggie and Granda in Book Two:

Maggie and the Magic Bookcase:
The Roman Rumpus

Coming soon to a bookcase near you!

CHECK OUT THE MAGIC BOOKCASE WEBSITE
FOR MORE INFORMATION AND EXCLUSIVE
CONTENT!

www.themagicbookcase.com

YOU CAN ALSO FIND MAGGIE AND GRANDA
ON SOCIAL MEDIA:

 The Magic Bookcase

 @tmagicbookcase

 @the_magic_bookcase

Lightning Source UK Ltd.
Milton Keynes UK
UKOW06f1204051017
310457UK00014B/739/P